Slow Burn

BETHANY RUTTER

CANDLEWICK PRESS

First US edition 2026
First published by Hot Key Books (UK) 2024

Library of Congress Control Number: pending
ISBN 978-1-5362-4383-3 (hardcover)
ISBN 978-1-5362-5164-7 (paperback)

25 26 27 28 29 30 SHD 10 9 8 7 6 5 4 3 2 1

Printed in Chelsea, MI, USA

This book was typeset in Berling LT Std.

Candlewick Press
99 Dover Street
Somerville, Massachusetts 02144

www.candlewick.com

EU Authorized Representative: HackettFlynn Ltd,
36 Cloch Choirneal, Balrothery, Co. Dublin, K32 C942, Ireland.
EU@walkerpublishinggroup.com

A JUNIOR LIBRARY GUILD SELECTION

For all the slowpokes

PROLOGUE

I'm dying. I'm sure of it. I'm literally going to EXPIRE right here, right now. Tell my mother I love her. And my dad and Sasha, and maybe Jake if you absolutely have to.

This run may be the death of me.

"Come on, slowpokes!" Mr. Pearce bellows. Is this the first time I've heard such a thing being yelled at me by a demonic PE teacher? No. Will it be the last? Also no. There he is, looking all smug, standing around with most of the class, including my various BFFs who all have anxious expressions as they witness my humiliation. The rest of them are just staring at us blankly like we're these weird curiosities.

We had been warned. I'll give him that. "Anyone who doesn't complete a lap of the playing field in less than three minutes will be made to do fifteen burpee star jumps," Mr. Pearce had told us. First and foremost, the word *burpee* is criminal in and of itself, and that's before we even get to the physical exertion required to *do* such a thing.

And I'm doing this *after* trying and failing to run a lap of the playing field in less than three minutes! In what world was I ever going to be able to do that? I might as well have just given up before I started. To be honest, I thought I was going to be the *only* one who failed, but here I am with Bolade and Sam, who also fall into the category of *slowpoke*. They're not fat and slow—they're just slow, which is less embarrassing overall but still pretty embarrassing because Mr. Pearce has *decided* to make it embarrassing.

"UGH!" I shout indignantly, but I carry on my torture and I feel the burn of (a) the unseasonably warm sun, (b) the eyeballs of my entire class (minus Sam and Bolade), (c) every muscle in my body, and (d) the perfectly calibrated humiliation of Mr. Pearce's PE lesson. What a way to finish the last day of my school year.

"There must"—Sam pants as he hauls himself up off the ground into a star jump—"be another way . . . to do this . . ."

"Do what?" Bolade asks, her eyes facing forward, determined, focused.

"PE . . . It doesn't need to . . . be like . . . this," he says.

"I'm . . . pretty . . . sure . . . it . . . does," I manage to utter breathlessly, unable to imagine a world in which PE is anything other than completely vile and embarrassing and frustrating.

"Nearly there. Come on, you lot! Ten more to go!" Mr. Pearce says in a tone that I think is meant to be rousing but just makes me want to karate kick him in the head.

I feel like I'm going to pass out right here and now. Ten more to go. My legs feel like they're going to give out, but I make them spring forward as springily as I can manage and then work my body into a star jump. Nine to go. Eight. Seven. Six—

"Ruby? Roo? Ruby! Wake up!" My best friend April's voice floats into my brain.

All I know is, I'm lying down and it's nice here. Nice on the ground. Nice not to be jumping around.

"Oh my days, is she *dead*?" Jessica sounds indignant, veritably furious at Mr. Pearce.

"I think she fainted!" That's Salma.

"Now, girls, please get out of the way."

I open my eyes to see Mr. Pearce's craggy visage looming above me. His sneer makes my humiliation boil over into rage. If my cheeks weren't already on fire from the relentless workout, I would be pink with fury. Sure, it's embarrassing, but more than anything, this kind of bullying just makes me *angry*. Like if the Incredible Hulk was a chubby sixteen-year-old girl. And not green.

"There you are, slowpoke. You're all right, aren't you? Nothing like a bit of a challenge to show you what you're really made of."

CHAPTER 1

"WURRRRRGH!" I emit not so much a scream as a strangled wail.

Whose idea was it to roller-skate in a park built on a hill? I think during the microsecond between losing my center of gravity and ending up on my bum. Someone falls over every time we go skating (except for Jessica, who hasn't fallen for weeks). And today it appears it's my turn!

"You all right, Roo?" Jessica skates over and holds out her hand to grab me, but I'm laughing too much to reply.

"I'm fine!" I finally say as she hauls me back to my feet with great elegance. "The benefits of extra padding." I run my hand over my bum and feel the place where it made impact with the ground, then skate over to where April and Salma are doing elegant laps, leaving Jessica to her more impressive backward skating that's drawing the attention of all the skateboarders at the nearby park. None of us had skated before Easter, but we all got a bit obsessed with watching videos and decided it just looked *too* fun. We had to wait for ages for skates that didn't cost a million pounds to come into stock in all our sizes, but that time came! And now we're a regular little roller-skating gang, zooming around without a care in the world since we've finished our exams.

Jessica is definitely the best. I guess gymnastics has given her an amazing center of gravity or something, but it's fantastic to watch, her long blue braids swinging behind her as she goes. She doesn't even wear kneepads or wrist guards. Then there's April, Salma, and me. April in her pure black skates with black wheels—she insisted on waiting until she could get them because she didn't want her skates messing with her look. And Salma and me in our matching pink pairs just doing our best. We've gone out a few times on the tennis court in Mayow Park when no one's booked it. A nice even surface for us to cruise around on. Find our footing. But Jessica had a need to live more dangerously, so here we are. On a hill.

"If you saw me fall on my bum . . . firstly, no you didn't. Secondly, erase it from your memory," I say, joining April and Salma.

"I feel like I'm about one second away from doing it myself," April says, clinging to Salma with her black-lace-gloved hands.

"Confidence!" Salma says, ever the optimist. "Don't let the skates smell your fear! They're like sharks or something."

"You're right," I say. "The second I feel nervous, that's when I do something weird and illogical with my feet and end up on the ground."

"We've all ended up on the ground at some point," Salma says encouragingly.

"But some of us are looking at the stars," April says with a sly smile.

Am I good at roller-skating? No. Is it fun? Yes. I haven't broken any bones so far, so I'm chalking that up as a win. Either way, it's just a good excuse to be outside on a sunny day with my pals.

I catch sight of Jessica talking to Joshua Jones from my history class. "Oh," I say, nodding toward the skate park. "*That's* why we're here."

"Good luck to her," April says, elegantly pressing the back of her wrist to her forehead to stop a droplet of sweat emanating from her blond pixie cut. Amid April's goth stylings, that's one thing she's always held out on. No black hair dye . . . yet.

"Why?" Salma asks. When she blinks, I can see the electric blue liquid eyeliner in a sharp strike across her eyelids. Truly a makeup mastermind. "He seems nice."

"Seems," April says, raising her eyebrows meaningfully.

"Oh, I see," I say, laughing. "So you don't actually know if there's anything wrong with Joshua; you just suspect it because there's no way there *isn't* something wrong with him."

"You know it, baby."

Jessica skates over to join us. "I am *obsessed* with him."

"Last week you said he was too much hard work," I remind her. "Too strong and silent. Or something?"

"I don't caaaaaare!" she says, throwing her arms wide and doing the roller-skating equivalent of a pirouette. "Nobody's perfect!"

"Well," Salma concedes, "you do look great together. But you said, literally with your own mouth, that you didn't think he was boyfriend material."

"He isn't, but I don't care!"

"I'm really appreciating the amount you're saying that you don't care," April says, grinning.

"It's because I don't!" Jessica says gleefully, high on the crush. "I'm just obsessed with him!"

"And I'm obsessed with your skating," I say.

I would *like* to be able to skate like Jessica, but for me, skating is purely for lols and japes, so I'm not going to sweat it too much that I'm not a pro.

"My goal is to be able to do the splits on skates by the end of the summer." She takes her phone out of the back pocket of her denim short-shorts to check the time. "Oh shit, I gotta go. Mum needs me to look after Marcus this afternoon. But, yeah, Operation Splits is *on*."

"Excited to find out how low you can go," April says as she plonks down on the metal bench to start unlacing her skates.

Jessica shrugs. "Practice makes perfect." Then she thinks for a moment. "No, wait . . . practice makes *better*."

"And will you just happen to do the splits in front of Joshua Jones?"

"Maybe I will, maybe I won't . . ." She winks and cackles devilishly.

We shove our skates in our bags (no *way* am I skating all the way home) and hug goodbye, Salma and Jessica heading up toward Crystal Palace as April and I take the nearby exit toward Sydenham.

CHAPTER 2

When we reach the little lot by the park, we gasp with delight. The ice cream van is there.

"How are they called a ninety-nine when they're never ninety-nine p?" April asks me in the queue.

"Maybe the ninety-nine doesn't refer to the price but instead to some mysterious cosmic force that makes them so delicious."

"It's possible. Definitely possible."

Once I've tapped my phone to pay the extortionate price of two ice creams, we leave the park and head toward home. It's so warm that my ice cream is already dripping onto my hand by the time we've crossed the main road next to the park.

"I think I would have died without an ice cream," April says, crunching the end of her wafer cone. "I'm not cut out for this."

"Yeah, I'm actually quite shocked that you came," I say. "Firstly, the sun, secondly . . ."

My words hang in the air. She doesn't answer. I nudge her with my hip.

"You know, you're allowed to talk about it. I *am* your best friend. If you can't talk to me about it, who can you talk to?"

"I don't want to talk to anyone! It's too shit. What's there to even talk about?"

"Fine." I sigh. "But I'm here if you want to talk about *you-know-who*."

"All right, all right," April says, waving the topic away. "Hey, do you want to go to the park? It's still kind of early."

We may have just *come* from a park, but when we say *the* park we mean Mayow Park. "Yeah, why not? I have nothing to do today, and the longer I'm out, the less I have to share physical space with Jake."

April shudders in horror. We continue our stroll under the hot afternoon sun. Eventually it becomes too much for April and she pulls her black mini parasol out of her backpack and rests it against her shoulder. The slightly ostentatious sight of someone dressed all in black with a black parasol catches the eye of a girl across the road walking a sausage dog in the opposite direction. April doesn't notice, so ensconced is she in her shady little goth oasis, but I realize it's Liv, aka The Other Fat Girl. We give each other a nod of acknowledgment.

Our school is pretty big, so I don't know everyone there by any means, and next year there'll be even *more* people I don't know—when we get an influx of new students for sixth form. But Liv's been there the whole time, and I can't honestly say that I know a thing about her, other than that she's, well, The Other Fat Girl. And that she appears to have a sausage dog. I know the word *fat* makes a lot of people prickle, but I'm pretty fine with it, so if she thinks, *Oh, there's Ruby, The Other Fat Girl*, I'm down with that. It's what I am. My feelings on the word are just one big shrug. But seeing her out and about makes me wonder . . . maybe it would be cool to have a fat friend. An ally. Or maybe she's all stressed out and self-hating and wouldn't *want* to be my friend. Who knows!

Finally we make it to Mayow Park and flop on the grass under a tree near the playground. April rests the parasol on the ground so it shields her face. We just chill on the grass, not saying anything. I've known April for long enough to be able to tell when she's in a quiet mood, and things not working out with Juliet have definitely left her a little more subdued than usual. The sound of summer is all around us. Some adults are playing softball in the big central grassy patch, the sound of ball hitting bat uniquely satisfying. Kids giggle as they go down the slide or get pushed on the swings. Intense-looking dudes use the outdoor exercise equipment. Sometimes a dog ambles over and sniffs around our little corner of the park with great interest.

"Ruby?" A voice cuts through the static summer air. Not April's—she's never sounded this bright and keen. I open my eyes under my heart-shaped sunglasses and sit up.

"Hi?" I say slowly, suspiciously, looking at this girl, who at first glance is a complete stranger, but then I recognize her from being a couple of years ahead of me at school. Pretty, blond, wearing extremely short shorts—so short, in fact, that the pockets are visibly poking out of the bottom.

"Oh, it *is* you!" she says, clearly delighted. "I'm Megan Harper. I don't know if you remember me from school? Anyway, I just wanted to say . . . tell your brother I said . . . hey." She looks embarrassed all of a sudden, her cheeks reddening.

"I will be sure to tell Jake that Megan Harper says hey," I tell her, smiling as sweetly as I can manage. "Maybe he'll drop you a message or something when I jog his memory."

Her face brightens again. "Oh, yes, maybe!"

We stare at each other in silence for a moment. April is still lying next to me, under her black parasol. No movement at all. Not so much as a twitch of an eyelid.

"Well," I say.

"I'll leave you to it . . ." Megan says.

"Yeah . . ."

She turns to walk away, then turns back a second later. "Don't forget!"

I lock my teeth in a rictus grin. "I won't!" I say with a cheeriness of such intense falsity that I'm sure she'll think I'm taking the piss. Which I am. If I could go one day of my life without someone fawning over my awful brother, I would be a happy Ruby Morgan. Then, finally, this Megan interloper is gone and April and I are alone again. Pretty much how we like it.

"Jesus." April chuckles, finally reanimating her immobile body.

"Tell me about it." I sigh and flop back onto the grass, trying to match the exact pattern of flattened greenery I'd left behind.

"Does that happen often?"

"I wouldn't go as far as to say *often*, but she's definitely not the first girl from his year who's greeted me with great enthusiasm and messages for the boy himself."

"Straight people are weird," she says, shaking her head slowly.

I shrug. "Some of us are OK."

"You'll do, I suppose." She resumes her position under the black-lace parasol. April may be a goth, but from the amount she avoids the sun, you would think she was an actual vampire. "So are you going to tell Jake that Megan Harper says hey?"

"Yeah. I feel sorry for anyone who fancies him because he's

such a dickhead. Which puts me in a bind, because either I don't tell him and I feel disloyal to the poor girl, or I do and she risks getting tangled up in some bullshit with him."

"A vile beast," April intones solemnly. "Is he still being a dick to Sasha?"

"Yeah." I sigh. "I mean, he's a dick to me too, but I mind it more when he's a dick to her. She's ten! Like, literally a baby! Leave her alone! She is a perfect little princess!"

"What's his latest crime?"

"Oh my God, so the other day my mum asked Sasha if she wanted to start getting her own breakfast in the morning over the holidays—a classic scam to make Sasha feel like a big girl and to save Mum the work when she already has loads to do—and this morning I came downstairs and Jake was standing there with her with the bowl of cereal on the digital kitchen scales and he was, like . . . taking cereal out of the bowl *flake by flake* until it was precisely the portion size stated on the box!"

April shudders. "Big, big yikes. What's the monster up to today?"

I don't even have to think about it. "Probably lifting weights in his room or shoehorning the fact that he goes to Oxford into whatever conversation he's having at the present moment."

"Classic Jake. Can you actually imagine wanting to work out on a day like today? *Wanting* to sweat?" April asks.

"Jesus, no. I can't imagine it at the best of times, and this is very much the worst of times."

It's a hot day at the end of June so we still have *loads* of the summer holidays left and the sunshine is feeling like a promise of more sunshine to come, nothing but blue skies from here until September. It doesn't matter if that doesn't come true. It's just that feeling of infinite possibility. Delicious.

"I'm still traumatized by memories of the bleep test, even though I know we don't have to do PE ever again." April sighs, bathing in the idyllic thought. "God bless sixth form."

"Yeah, but . . . you always did fine at stuff like that," I say, frowning.

"I disagree with it *on principle*. Like, *politically*. It seemed like it was designed to make us all feel like shit. It's not even . . . *the law* or the curriculum. It's just something Mr. Pearce wanted to do to assert his dominance. Remember what he was like with *you* with those sprints?"

Just the mention of that cursed lesson has got my blood boiling. Of *course* I remember the sprints! It was the most humiliating thing ever! Mr. Pearce decided I wasn't running fast enough when the class was doing timed sprints, so he made me run on my own in front of everyone while the rest of them took a break. Can you imagine? I was scarlet with cringe. Pure humiliation. All those eyes on my fat body, and me just trying my best but not being as good as everyone else, which to him *obviously* meant I wasn't trying. It was on that day that I knew I was *never* going to enjoy exercise. Nope. Not the one.

"Well, all that is behind us," I say, throwing my arms wide, ending the PE chat right there. "Isn't life so much better now that we're headed into sixth form?"

"One million percent. And you know what's even better than sixth form?"

"What?"

"Summer holiday before sixth form."

"*So* true."

"We get to do nothing. Nothing!"

"Summer of chill," I say, reaching lazily behind me for my water bottle. And chill is exactly what I need. Maybe a little roller-skating and watching horror movies with April and Salma and Jessica. Maybe a little helping my mum with her baking business, maybe a little doing nothing with April, just the way we like it.

Except this summer feels different. No Dad.

Well, it's not like he's *dead* or anything. But not having him around is weird. Manchester's not the ends of the earth, but it's not the end of the block either. It's easy to forget he's gone sometimes because the rest of us are still here, so it just seems logical that he is too. But then you realize his stuff isn't here anymore, and, oh yeah, you remember hugging him goodbye at the end of the garden path a few months ago, and yes, he really is gone. Five became four.

CHAPTER 3

When I've stomped back home from the park, down the road with the big white blossom trees and over the railway bridge, I can hear Jake banging about in his room in the loft. I'm angling to take over his room now that he's at university, but the negotiations haven't quite come to fruition yet. I just think it's ridiculous that he's hanging on to the biggest room and he doesn't even live here anymore! Seems like he gets his own way a *lot* just by refusing to engage with other people. Couldn't be me! I *love* to engage.

I knock on the door and wait to be admitted into my brother's sacred space. Once I hear a reluctant "Come in," followed by the clanging of a weight being deposited back into its rack, I enter. The room is pretty big, but it feels as if his rack of weights takes up about half of it. There's a pull-up bar over the door where in his pre-university days he could be seen raising and lowering himself using only his upper-body strength.

"What do you want, Freckle Face?" Jake asks impatiently. He settles onto the bed and waits for me to speak.

"A girl called Megan told me to tell you hey," I say, just so I've been true to my word.

Jake looks pensive for a moment, moving his chiseled jaw from side to side as he thinks. "Fit Megan?" he says finally.

"Megan Harper. Long blond hair."

"Huh." Jake nods slowly. "I'm glad you said her and not that absolute cow Megan Cross. Fit Megan, eh?" He reaches for an open bag of Maltesers on his bedside table and tosses one high in the air before catching it in his mouth.

"Yeah . . . Although I'm sure Megan Cross is, in fact, a total babe," I say.

Jake scoffs. "You would say that. You're such a 'feminist,'" he says, putting air quotes around *feminist*.

I roll my eyes. "Yes . . . and?"

"And it means you're obviously going to stand up for any random girl!"

"That's . . . literally not what feminism means." Would it shock you to learn this is not the first time I've had to go over this with my brother?

"Anyway, what else did she say?" He doesn't look at me, instead he throws another Malteser in the air and catches it in his mouth.

"Nothing." I shrug.

"All right. Not like I'm short on girls now that I'm working behind the bar . . . but always good to know anyway."

"Glad to hear your social standing has increased now that you've graduated from collecting glasses to pulling pints," I say, but he's not listening.

He sticks out his chin in a thoughtful pose and I wait for him to say something else. He looks at me as if to ask why I'm still in his room. "You can go now." Ah, definitely worth waiting for!

I sigh. "Fine."

But as I turn to go, a shiny thing hanging from one of the posts on his bed frame catches my eye. Two shiny things, in fact.

"Why do you have two Dawson Dash medals? You only won it once."

Jake looks up at me like he can't believe I'm still in here, sucking up his oxygen. "One's mine, one's Dad's. I asked him if I could keep it when he was sorting his stuff out for . . ." His eyes scan the room, still not sure how to say it. "You know, for moving out." I feel a momentary twinge of sympathy for Jake. We're all a bit beaten down by our parents splitting up, but it must feel especially weird for Jake. He was away at university for the past year so he missed the worst of it, and it feels like he doesn't really believe it got as bad as it did.

"Oh," I say, shrugging, wanting to deflect the conversation away from our dad's absence. "I didn't know he won."

Jake scowls at me. "How did you not know that? Everyone knows. That's why it was such a big deal for him when I won it two years ago. Making it a family tradition or something."

"OK, this rings a bell," I concede, even though it doesn't. Dawson is a *sporty* school, always beating other local schools at football and rugby and hockey and netball and athletics. Which obviously does *not* appeal to me since zero effort is made to include people like yours truly who might want to take part even if they're not very good. It's for Real Competitors only.

"Of course *you* weren't paying any attention to that," he mutters.

Why would I be paying attention to the Dawson Dash? A race invented about a million years ago as an act of charity by St. Alfred's (very fancy) toward our school (Dawson High, not so fancy) whereby they let us use their absurdly huge playing fields but *only* outside of term time. Because they're nice like that. We have our own outdoor space now! It's the twenty-first century! But somehow the tradition persists, because everyone's decided it's *important*. I guess that's what tradition is.

"Oh, did you not get enough praise and attention from elsewhere for winning the stupid race?" I say in a tone I know he'll find infuriating.

"It's not stupid! It's *prestigious*."

Yeah, maybe amid the fascist PE contingent it is.

"And anyway, you win *actual* money now," Jake says, tossing and catching another Malteser in his mouth. It's true. There's a £100 prize for the winner, £75 for silver, and £50 for bronze. Actual money. I told you—sports are a serious business at Dawson. "You only think it's stupid because you could never win it."

I fold my arms across my chest and look at him intently. "Why couldn't I?"

"You mean other than the fact that I've never seen you run for the bus let alone five kilometers? And the fact that you're *massively* out of shape?" he says, with emphasis on the *massively*, eyeing me with a mix of skepticism and mild distaste. "Just plain massive."

Jake lacks the art of subtlety, you know? Any normal person would have left it there, but he has to go right ahead and make it *explicit*.

"Why do you always have to be such a dick?"

But before he can answer, we're interrupted.

"What are you two arguing about?" Sasha's round face appears in the doorframe. She's like a moth to the flame. Not to mention the fact that her bedroom is next to my mum's on the first floor, so her presence upstairs in the loft is very indicative of her commitment to being where the action is all the time.

"Go away, Chunk." Jake sighs. If you thought he looked down on *me,* wait until you see how little time he has for our ten-year-old sister!

"Can I have a Malteser?" she says, spying the red bag on the bedside table.

"No."

"Why not?"

"Because they're bad for you."

"Why are you allowed them?" she asks indignantly.

I can tell where this is headed.

"Because I work out and *you* do not."

Sasha frowns. "OK," she says a little sadly. "What were you two talking about?"

"Jake was just being mean to me," I say, not wanting to go into the details of it with her. Yes, she can be annoying, but I've taken it upon myself to try to prevent her from hearing anything that might make her feel self-conscious about her body or believe there's anything she can't do. Her body seems to bother Jake just as much as mine does.

"Why?" she asks.

"I don't know," I say, shrugging and hoping she will slope off back downstairs to watch TV.

"I was telling Ruby why she wouldn't be able to win the Dawson Dash," Jake says, back on his bicep curls.

Damn it. Irritation flares in my chest.

"What's that?"

Jake sighs impatiently. "You know Dawson? The school you're going to go to the year after next? It's their annual race for the sixth form. Don't you remember? I won it two years ago? You were there?"

"It's just a silly tradition thing," I say. "It's been going for years. You have to run five kilometers in a route that goes around the St. Alfred's playing fields. You know, near where those horses are, by the park."

Sasha thinks about it. "Why wouldn't she?"

"Why wouldn't she what?"

"Be able to win," Sasha says, who clearly holds me in such high esteem that it's never crossed her mind that I wouldn't be able to win a race. If only everyone else saw me through Sasha's eyes, then I would be on to a win.

Jake looks at her like she's insane. "Because she can't even run to the end of the road! Because she's f—"

"Enough of this! I'm going to do it," I say with a decisive clap of my hands, cutting him off. Yes, I *am* fat, but Sasha doesn't need to hear it getting hurled around as an insult, like a weapon. How's she ever going to have a chill relationship with her body if she has to listen to that in her own home?

"Oh, ha, ha, very funny," Jake says, setting the dumbbell back on its rack and pulling a face at me.

"I'm not joking," I say, my expression a mask of sincerity. "I'll do it."

"Oh, you will, will you?" He looks vaguely amused.

"Yeah," I say, fixing him with a stare as if I'm dead serious. "Family tradition."

He laughs. "You think you're on a level with me and Dad?"

I nod. Might as well.

"I think you can do it!" says Sasha. Of course she does. I'm her big sister.

"Well, well, well," he says. "Now, this I would like to see."

When is race day? September the fifth? That rings a bell. He'll have forgotten all about it by then. I just don't want him thinking he can walk all over me just because he's Mr. Macho Athlete, captain of the Dawson rugby team, Oxford Rowing Shithead. None of that means anything to me!

"Good, well, that's settled, then," I say. "Come on, Sasha. Let's go play *Luigi's Mansion*."

As we're trailing down the stairs, Jake calls after me. "You're not going to get fit playing on the Switch all summer!"

"Thanks, but I don't need your advice!" I call back.

Sinking into the sofa with Sasha and watching her hoover up ghosts on a video game isn't exactly the most thrilling way to spend an hour, but I'm desperate to make her feel loved and looked after.

She pauses the game and sighs dramatically, but I can tell something's actually up. "I miss Dad."

I clear my throat, wondering what to say. "What do you miss about him?"

She thinks for a minute. "I miss . . . playing football with him in the park."

"You could always do that with me or Jake. Just ask if you want to," I offer. I know that was their thing—Sasha loves playing football, and Dad did everything he could to encourage her—but I don't want her to just stop now that he's moved out.

"Maybe . . ." she says thoughtfully. "And I miss having pizza on Wednesdays. We haven't done that for ages."

"We could do that."

"It wouldn't be the same."

"No, but it might be all right?"

"But yeah . . . I just miss him."

I squeeze her to me in an awkward sideways hug. "Me too."

As if the touch of my hug set something off inside her, she looks up at me and asks, "Do you think my arms are too squishy?"

I swallow. "No. I think they're the perfect amount of squishy. Why?"

She shrugs. "They're squishier than everyone else's."

"Do you mind that?"

She looks like she's really thinking about it, but maybe it's just her concentrating on the video game. "I don't know." She chews on the ends of her hair for a moment, which is disgusting and ordinarily I would poke her and tell her to stop, but I don't want to interrupt her. "Do you think that's why Jake doesn't like me?"

That makes my heart drop. Properly.

"Don't be silly. Of course he likes you! He's just being a horrible elder brother. That's all. And I don't think you're too squishy. Or too anything. And if anyone's making you feel like this, then just . . . tell me and we can talk about it, yeah?" I hear a creak on the stairs behind us and then the almost imperceptible sound of retreating footsteps. Jake. At least he knows when he's not wanted.

"Yeah," she says, and nods. But I don't know if she will. Especially if, to quote the horror films April and I love to freak ourselves out with, *the call is coming from inside the house.*

Over dinner that evening, I keep looking at Sasha from across the table, wondering how it is that she's ten years old and already worrying about her body. I wonder when it starts. How it starts. I wish I could remember how old I was when I first knew my body was *wrong* somehow. I chose to kick back against that idea and not let it completely gnaw away at my life, but what if Sasha can't? What if this is just the beginning of something that's going to steal her time and her energy and push her into limiting what she chooses to do with herself? The thought makes me shiver.

"You all right, Roo?" Mum asks.

"Yeah, I'm fine," I say.

"You looked really spaced out!" she says, laughing.

"She was probably daydreaming of a feminist utopia," Jake says, clearly undeterred by having overheard a conversation between his sisters about what a hostile presence he is.

I point my fork at him across the table and close one eye like I'm a hunter taking aim at my prey. "You know it."

The shrill tone of the home phone ringing cuts through the dining room. We all sit there, looking shiftily at each other, waiting for someone to pick it up.

"Oh, all right," Mum says, getting to her feet and padding into the living room.

"Hello? Oh, hi . . ." Even with only a few words and half the conversation, I can tell it's Dad. We can all tell it's Dad. Just something about the shift in tone in my mum's voice. A shift in the atmosphere. "Yeah, we're fine. We're just eating at the moment. You all right?" A pause. "That's good. I'm glad you're settling in there. Well, we're sort of halfway through dinner, but if you call back in a bit, they'll be able to talk." Another pause. "Oh, you are. Hope it's somewhere nice. Well, why don't you try them on their mobiles tomorrow? OK. Fine. Speak to you soon, then. Bye."

When she returns to the table, Jake instantly asks, "Why didn't you let us speak to him?"

"Because we're eating! I told him that!" Mum says, resuming her spaghetti.

"It doesn't matter. I would have spoken to him."

"And then your food would have gotten cold, so no. If you're that bothered, why don't you ring him on your mobile?"

Jake shrugs.

"Well, then," she says, settling the matter. But a cloud descends on the dinner table after that. An awkwardness.

It feels like I've only been asleep for a few minutes that night when the smell of cigarette smoke floats into my room. Is Jake smoking in the loft? It would be just like him to try to get us all killed. I creep out onto the landing and turn my head toward the short flight of stairs up to his room. I can't smell it anymore. I go back into my room and realize it's coming from outside. When I put my face to the window and look out, I see my mum huddled in her dressing gown and slippers, sitting on the low wall in our front garden, illuminated by the security light. She's crying. Just letting the tears run down her face as she smokes. I didn't even *know* she smoked. Maybe it's a new thing. The sight turns my stomach over. Should I go down and talk to her? Or would she be embarrassed about it? I don't know what to do or which is right. I stand there, nibbling my lip. Just as I decide I'll go downstairs and ask if she's OK, I see her get up, stub the cigarette out on the wall, and go back inside. I don't even hear the door closing behind her, that's how quiet she's being. Maybe I was right not to interrupt.

CHAPTER 4

Did I only see April yesterday? Maybe. Is she at my house now? I couldn't possibly say.

We're lying on the grass in the front garden, across the stone path from where Mum was sitting last night. When I woke up this morning, I wondered if I had dreamed it. But the feeling was too real. And besides, why wouldn't she have been smoking and crying on her own in the middle of the night? I keep wondering whether to bring it up with her, but the thought of it fills me with a deep well of cringe. The real question is how many times she's been out there and I *haven't* heard. I'll just settle for being extra nice to her and hope that's enough.

April is lying on her back, reading a battered secondhand copy of *The Bell Jar*. I'm lying on my front, wearing my heart-shaped sunglasses and consuming the panels of *The Diary of a Teenage Girl*. Eventually I put it down, roll over, and just let the sun warm me. The grass is tickling the backs of my thighs in my cutoff denim shorts, but there's something so deliciously summery about the feeling that I don't want to move.

After a silence, I take a deep breath. I may not be able to speak to my mum about what I saw last night, but I can definitely check in with my best friend, however reluctant she is to talk. "I know you don't like talking about your feelings but . . . humor me. Are you doing OK?"

April growls like a dog and rolls over onto her front. "Yes and no," she says finally.

"Tell me more."

"Yes in that I will live and no in that I wish Juliet and I were still together."

I sigh. "I'm sorry. I wish there was something I could do to make you feel better. What's the point of a best friend if I can't do that?"

"Yeah!" April says, flicking my arm and grinning. "What's even the point of you?"

Our discussion is cut short by the sight of a moving van pulling up outside my house. It gives me a sick feeling in the pit of my stomach. A repetition of a not-very-distant memory. My dad's slow, morose march to and from the van, which was much smaller than this but still looked half empty with his things inside. No one gets out of the van, which is weird but also means we can resume our chat in the absence of anything more interesting to look at.

"Anyway," April says, "I heard Juliet is going out with Rosie Wood, so it's all pointless anyway. I've just got to get over it."

"Poor bro," I say, stroking her blond pixie cut.

"It's fine. There are plenty more fish in the sea or whatever," she says, but I can tell that things not working out with Juliet has wounded her. The roles have never been reversed, though. I've never done breakup moping with support from April because I've never had a relationship. In fact, I've been kind of avoiding it. Not that I haven't had crushes, but I've never felt ready to put myself *out there* like that. It sounds properly horrible. "Did you tell Jake about that girl from the park?"

"I did, and he barely knew who I was talking about. Pathetic!"

"Is he still being horrible to Sasha?"

"Oh yes, he is. He refused to give her a Malteser on the grounds that she doesn't exercise. He is an absolute menace to society."

April is indignant. "She's ten!"

"I know! He keeps trying to get her to do those computer games that are actually exercise! Like, he's obsessed. It's as if he knows he's not going to win against me, so he's moved on to terrorizing Sasha."

Just then, a car pulls up and the doors to the moving van open almost simultaneously. Out of the car come three people, a man and a woman and a younger guy, maybe my age, and the moving crew gets to work, unloading boxes and hauling out a bed frame. As the older man approaches the front door of the house next to ours, examining various keys, the boy is looking around at his new surroundings. Tall, slim but broad-shouldered, in a white T-shirt and black jeans with skate shoes . . . From what I'm able to ascertain from this preliminary spying, he's actually pretty . . . cute. I catch a glimpse of the woman's face and wonder where I know her from. Is she a teacher at my school? Maybe she works at Sainsbury's or something. The recognition is faint, but it's there.

"I feel weird lying here while those guys are, like, killing themselves hauling that stuff out of the van," April says, springing to her feet. "Let's go inside."

I'm disappointed at the interruption—I want to know more about the boy—but I do what she says. We shout a hello to Sasha, who's lying in front of the TV, and to Mum, who's working on some orders in the kitchen. Mum tries to engage us in conversation, but we're on business. Important spying business. We head up to my room, which is at the front of the house and looks out onto the street. We watch the movers empty the van: a stylish sofa turned on its side to fit through the door, a sturdy-looking chest of drawers—not something flat-pack from IKEA—a bike. And then the boy reappears. He perches on the end of the wall that divides our front garden from theirs, playing on his phone. But the sun is so bright that he swivels around to cast a shadow over the phone, turning toward my house.

Even from a distance, I can tell that my initial assessment of *cute* was not wrong. Now that I can look at him for longer, I take him in. Thick, messy dark red hair. Full lips. A face that's got a touch of sweetness mixed in with the overall hot. I feel that light bubbling sensation in my chest. That inconvenience of a crush announcing itself. But amid the fizzing excitement, there's some strand of familiarity there too.

"Hey," says April, her elbows resting on the windowsill, her chin on her upturned palms. "I think I know him."

"That guy?"

"Yeah. Oliver, I think. Oliver Cowan."

"Where from?"

"I think maybe, like, Scouts?"

"Oooh, like, *back in the day*. Tell me all!"

But then, before she can answer, Oliver glances up at the window. No! Pure horror! Maybe our surveillance tactics need a little bit of work. He squints up for a split second, like he isn't sure we're really there. "Get down!" I hiss, pulling April to the floor where we dissolve into giggles. When our laughter subsides, my curiosity does not.

"Hey, doofus," I say, nudging her from our slumped position. "What's the intel on him?"

"I dunno. Can't tell you much. All I remember is he went to St. Alfred's Prep." She sits up, leaning against the bed frame. "Why? You got a lil crush? You got a lil thing for gingers?"

"Not now that I know he went to St. Alfred's." I mime puking, trying to throw her off the subject.

"Why so interested, then?" She raises her eyebrows in a *gotcha* face.

"No reason," I say as casually as I can affect.

"You know, you're allowed to fancy people," April says.

"What's that supposed to mean?" I'm a little taken aback because . . . well, I'm just a bit surprised that she's managed to read me like this.

"Whenever you have a crush, it's like . . ." She gestures in her black-lace fingerless gloves, trying to find the right words. "It's like you're all guilty and embarrassed about it, even though it's, like, totally normal. It's as if you think there's something shameful about it, for *you* in particular."

I feel my face go red. "No . . . it's . . . not . . ." I begin, but I don't really know how I plan to continue. Because I know she's right. Ugh, the mortifying ordeal of being known!

"It's OK," she says breezily. "I just don't think you need to feel like that."

"It's just very cringe and demoralizing, you know," I say, realizing it's OK to talk about this with April. "I feel weird about fancying people because I'm like . . . why would they ever be interested in me? So it becomes all one-sided and weird."

"They would be interested in you because you're bitchin'," she reassures me. "But I get it. I mean, I don't exactly get it, but I know what you're saying."

"It's, like, I'm pretty chill about my body, but there are just these little *things* that are poking at me and stressing me out. And I don't want them to! I just want to live in peace! Live my fully glorious life!"

"I hear you. For what it's worth, I think maybe you do yourself down. Like, remember when you fancied that guy in your history class?"

"Unfortunately, yes," I say grimly, remembering Angus Moore.

"See! You're always so negative about this stuff, but I think he really did like you! Remember when he asked you if you were going to Harry's party?"

I shrug. "Yeah, well, I wasn't. I was hanging out with you and Salma."

"The fact is, he did still ask! But you're just so convinced that no one will like you that you couldn't even contemplate it."

"You *really* thought Angus liked me?" I remain unconvinced but am at least a little interested in her hypothesis.

"I don't know—I can't read his mind! But all I know is that there was no evidence that he definitely *didn't* like you, but you seemed to think it was a foregone conclusion. You sabotage! So if you do like Oliver Cowan, then you're allowed to admit it! I promise you."

I exhale loudly. "Fine. I think he's cute," I mumble. "I'm not, like, in love with him, though! I only just saw him! All I'm saying is that he's cute."

"And that's enough for me," April says, clapping her hands together. "Oliver Cowan is your new crush. I'm certifying it." She mimes stamping a piece of paper.

That familiarity again. I concentrate really hard, saying his name aloud.

"What, is that like a spell? Are you doing some kind of love spell? I didn't think you were into witchy shit." April is eyeing me with suspicion.

"No . . . I'm just trying to place it. It's like I knew that name a long time ago, but I can't think why . . ." I scrunch up my face trying to mine my memories. And there it is! "Ollie Cowan! He was my little mate in nursery school! Even before I met *you*."

"Huh!" April says. "But you didn't recognize him?"

"Oddly enough, he's changed a bit since he was four . . ."

"How does this affect the crush situation? Positively? Negatively?"

"Neutral, I think? It's not really anything, is it?"

She shrugs. "Not really."

We play cards on my bedroom floor for an hour before she heads home, but the whole time I'm running over what she said. Fine, I can admit that I think Ollie is cute, but I also don't think I would ever stand a chance with him. Clearly this isn't something I'm going to fix overnight.

CHAPTER 5

Mum's peering into the fridge. Her big blond topknot is providing a buffer against the top of the fridge, and she's very clearly stressed out. She's rummaging furiously among the glass jars on the top shelf. "God!" she exclaims.

"What's up?" I'm not convinced whatever the answer is will match her level of anxiety.

"I thought we had pickled jalapeños and now I find we have none! How am I meant to make quesadillas without them?" She looks bereft. Little things seem to be piling on top of her these days. "They have four ingredients! And we don't have one of them! That's a quarter of the ingredients, Roo! Twenty-five percent!"

I shrug, attempting to downgrade the seriousness of this dilemma from "life-threatening" to "minor inconvenience."

"I can go and get us some."

Relief floods her face. "Would you?"

"Yeah, it's fine. I'm not even doing anything." When am I ever?

She looks at the clock on the oven. "Can you go now, please? I don't want us to be eating dinner really late," Mum pleads.

"All right, all right, since you're desperate," I say, shoving my feet into some flip-flops and grabbing a shopping bag out of the shopping bag that's overflowing with shopping bags. I hold out my hand for some cash, and she duly drops a few pounds into my chubby palm. "They're not going to have them in the dinky little Sainsbury's by the station, so I'll walk to the big one."

"You're a good girl." Yes, Mum. Yes I am. "And if you do that, I'll have time to give the new neighbors a box of my brownies as a welcome gift. I just baked some when I saw the moving van. Thought it would be nice, you know."

"Do you remember my little ginger friend Ollie from nursery school?"

She thinks for a minute, twitching her nose in concentration. "Yes!" she says finally. "God, I had completely forgotten about him! Oh, you two were so sweet. I would have to drag you out of nursery school because you wanted to keep playing with him."

"Well, he and his parents are the ones who moved in next door," I say.

"How funny! Did you recognize him? After all this time?"

"No. April said she had been in Scouts with him, but it was only when she said his name that I remembered."

She shakes her head. "Oliver Cowan. Well, I can't remember if he likes brownies, but I've got to go around there either way."

"*And* it's always nice to source potential new customers."

"That's the last thing I need right now! I can barely keep up with the customers I have already!" She sighs. It's another one of the many things that are stressing her out. She got fed up with paying fees to have a stall at the market in Crystal Palace Park, so she decided to go out on her own and just sell through Instagram a few months ago. Things are going just as well, and she doesn't have to contend with the elements and having enough cash for the change float and all these other things she learned you have to think about when you're doing a market. I much prefer it like this because I used to get roped in to helping her and I hated standing around in the cold, hoping that one day I would regain the feeling in my hands. But I do like helping her. I'm proud of her running her own business, whether that's in real life or online.

"Maybe I can help you if you need it? Oh, and maybe when I get back we can talk about the bedroom situation . . . ?" I say over my shoulder as I leave.

When I head out into the evening air, it's still light out and there are children playing on the estate across the road from our house. Everything feels peaceful. I start walking to the main road, trying to inject a little urgency into my pace.

At the end of the street, I have two options: one, walk along the main road and around the bend until I get to the supermarket, which is longer; two, walk up Round Hill and down the other side, which is shorter. Obviously I would rather *not* walk up the hill, but Mum did seem pretty stressed out about dinner. Hill it is.

I embark on my quest. Now, Round Hill isn't a gentle incline. It's *steep*. So steep I don't think I've ever even seen anyone cycling down it for fear of getting catapulted into oncoming traffic when they get to the bottom.

Every step feels like a punishment, pain searing through my legs and my lungs burning with the effort. Jesus Christ, what planet was I even on when I said I could win the Dawson Dash? Planet Delusional. I love moving my cute little bod with some roller-skating, but this is very much something else. My calves are about to give out by the time I get to the top and I'm properly gasping for air.

But I made it. I made it. I'm panting and leaning against a letter box when a little white Scottie dog comes sniffing at my ankles. I bend to greet it, my breath still ragged, when its owner appears, looming above me. Mr. Pearce. The demon PE teacher. What's a demon doing with such a cute dog? Shouldn't be allowed.

"Hello, Ruby," he says, surveying me disdainfully as usual. It's weird he even remembers my name since there's no way I was what you could call a star pupil in his lessons. Even though it's summer and decidedly not sweatshirt weather, he's still wearing his classic uniform of a sweatshirt over a polo shirt with shorts and trainers, socks pulled up for maximum visibility. A PE-teacher look for all seasons—are they issued with this when they emerge from the womb fully formed as PE teachers?

"Hi, Mr. Pearce," I say reluctantly, still panting a little. Or a lot. The hill is no joke!

"Are you . . . all right?"

"Yes, fine. Just stomped up the hill a bit too fast. Just trying to catch my breath."

He looks at me for a moment, like he's contemplating whether to speak. "You know, if you didn't have *quite* so much meat on your bones, it wouldn't be so difficult for you to get from A to B."

I glare at him. I was quite used to all his fat-shaming in PE classes, but I shouldn't have to listen to it in the summer holidays. "Wow, what an insightful tip. I'll bear that in mind," I say, cocking my head sarcastically. It reminds me of when he used to shout "Come on, slowpoke!" at me from the other end of the gym when we would do the bleep test or basically anything that required me to move with any haste. Ugh! I can still hear it echoing around my skull! Horrible.

"You *don't* need to take that tone with me, Ruby Morgan." And then, as if saying my name brought something back to him: "You should take a leaf out of your brother's book. Now, there's a real athlete—I heard he's rowing at Oxford now, hmmm?"

Ah, I see. That's why he remembers me. The great mystery: how Jake and Ruby Morgan share any genetic material at all.

"You heard right," I say, shrugging. "Well, I've got to go now." I stomp off in the direction of Sainsbury's before he fawns over Jake more. It's like Jake's brainwashed everyone into thinking he's great! He's not great! He's a dick!

Under a cloud of irritation, I complete my task. The jalapeños are bought, and dinner is saved! On the way home, I don't go back via Round Hill. Instead I take the longer route along the main road so as not to stand any chance of bumping into Mr. Pearce again. I've never really understood why people have to be quite *brazen* with their opinions about my body: what's wrong with it, how they propose to fix it. I've never asked for them. In fact, I'm just trying to merrily live my life and do what I want against a tidal wave of shit. It shouldn't be this hard! The closer I get to home, the more annoyed I feel by it all. Why does Jake get to be the golden child while he's effectively *terrorizing* his sister? Not me—I'm fine—but Sasha! What about her?

Screw it. If Jake thinks the idea of me running the race is a big joke, I'll show him just how wrong he is. If Mr. Pearce thinks I need to lose some of the "meat on my bones" in order to "get from A to B," then I'll show him that me *and* my meaty bones are capable of not just getting from A to B but winning the Dawson Dash. If Sasha is ten years old and already worrying about her sweet, perfect body, then I'm going to show her she can do anything she wants, on her own terms, in the body she has.

CHAPTER 6

After dinner I go to my room and systematically throw things out of my wardrobe, praying that I still have my trainers. And there, skulking at the back of the wardrobe, is my old PE kit. I tip it out onto the floor and retrieve the trainers, then put on a T-shirt and leggings. Maybe I need a sports bra? Well, too late for that now—we're going to work with what we've got. I creep downstairs as quietly as humanly possible. My secret shame! My mum is watching TV in the living room, and as I open the front door, I call to her, "I'm just going out for a bit, but I'll be back soon!" I hear her shout back, asking where I'm going, but I don't want her to see me in the running gear.

On the doorstep, I take out my phone and text April.

> ACCOUNTABILITY CHECK! First thing: Don't laugh. This is not a joke. I am entering the Dawson Dash. Jake is being a dickhead and then I bumped into Mr. Pearce 😮 who basically fat-shamed me, and I'm sick of the lot of them and I want to show Sasha all the cool shit she can do.

Her reply is instant.

Spite is as good a motivator as any. You got this.

Even though I'm buoyed by April's support, when I head down the garden path, it hits me that I have no idea what I'm doing. I guess I'm . . . running, right? So I should just . . . do that? Start? At the end of the path, I break into a run. Pounding the pavement, pumping my arms, going as fast as I can. And that means . . . I'm running! I'm running! I'm really doing it! Maybe it's not so hard after all? Only thing is, my bra isn't doing much. There's an *intense* jiggle going on that's bordering on painful.

But no matter! We have to look at the bigger picture! There I am, bouncing merrily along Sydenham Park Road at great speed, wondering where my run is going to take me next! Running! And then something . . . doesn't feel right. At all. It's like all my insides are jangled up, my quesadillas sitting somewhere in my chest rather than down in my stomach. Oh no. This is bad. This is very no bueno. I stop, panting, outside one of the huge, fancy double-fronted houses with a gravel drive. And there, leaning over, trying desperately to catch my breath and get my insides under control again, I vomit. I won't go into details, but suffice to say those hard-won pickled jalapeños made a comeback.

Oh God. That was decidedly not the one. First lesson learned: No running straight after dinner. That way vomiting lies. Second lesson learned: Turns out I do need a sports bra.

Amid all the internal and external jiggling, what really hits me is the feeling of those first, er, twenty seconds? That was . . . good. That felt powerful. I felt powerful. And maybe I can capture that again. It's clear I don't have a clue what I'm doing. But maybe I can learn. It's like school. I can learn anything I need to, as long as I commit to it, focus, have the right materials and a bit of guidance. The guidance . . . now that's something to think about. Maybe I need to enlist a little help.

As I'm standing doubled over on the pavement, face-to-face with my dinner, I hear the pounding of feet on the pavement approaching me. I look up, and to my absolute horror it's Ollie in a pair of *extremely* short shorts. He gives me a goofy little wave of acknowledgment as he passes, before doing a double take and circling back. Shit!

"Uh . . ." he says, frowning at me. "Are you all right?"

For a moment I contemplate pretending that it's not *me* who threw up but some other random person, and I'm just, you know, inspecting it. "I'm fine!" I say breezily. "Are you?"

"Well, I'm not the one who just . . ." He gestures vaguely at the ground.

"Oh that! No, nothing to worry about! Everything is fine!"

"Sure?" he says, raising his straight thick eyebrows expectantly. It's clear he doesn't recognize me, which is perfectly understandable since I didn't strictly recognize him either. I wonder if I should say anything. But before I can say a word about our shared past or even reassure him that I'm fine, I feel that familiar churning, burning in my chest and within a split second I'm throwing up again. As it hits the pavement, it narrowly misses his trainers that, even from my upside-down angle, look extremely profesh next to my battered "white" canvas plimsolls. He leaps back a foot. Quite understandably.

"Oh . . . my God," I say in complete disbelief, standing up again. I look at him in pure shock. "I'm so sorry!"

"Don't apologize to me!" he says. "Come on, let's get you

home." We start back down the road. I don't know what I was expecting from him based on a few minutes of spying, but he's much . . . nicer than I thought? As if hot people can't also be nice! Is that a thing? Either way, I'm glad he's nice, but also, what chance do I have of suppressing my crush now?!

"You don't have to come with me, you know. I'm not going to pass out on the way there. Look," I say, pointing. "There! I can see my house from here."

"I know where you live. I saw you in the garden when we moved in yesterday. Do you think I would have offered to walk you home if you lived any farther?" He smiles good-naturedly.

I seize the moment. "Hey, sorry, um, I don't know if you, uh, remember me . . . like, at all. Obviously it's been a long time, so you probably don't, but . . . I think we were, like, in nursery school together?" I say in a moment of uncharacteristic awkwardness.

He turns his head and looks at me as we walk. "Were we?"

"Yeah . . . Ruby?"

And then a smile spreads across his face. "Ruby! God, I had completely forgotten you! No offense, I mean."

"No, it was the same for me at first!"

"How weird . . ." He smiles. "Yeah, I remember you now. You always wore the brightest colored clothes."

"Ha! Baby fashion queen. Sounds about right." I'm glad it wasn't all a figment of my imagination. "I'm sorry for interrupting your run," I say, grimacing.

He shrugs. "It's fine. I'll just head out again. So do you run too?" I feel like we're walking very slowly. Even though it's only a short distance from the scene of my crime to my front door, it seems like it's taking a long time, like one or both of us is deliberately going slow.

"No, that was my first attempt. But I clearly timed it all wrong . . ."

"The human body is a strange little machine, isn't it?"

"Tell me about it."

When we get to our two houses sitting side by side, he says to me, "You know, if you ever want some help or whatever, just ask. You know where to find me." He nods at the house on the right.

"Thanks," I say, wondering if he really means it or if he's just trying to be polite or if he's just flexing some macho muscle. "Hope you have a good run!"

He nods at me and then turns back toward the road, setting off in a light jog, like it's nothing. And maybe it is nothing for him! But I'm used to being . . . good at things? So to be bad at something is very jarring!

"Where have you been?" Mum calls from the living room.

"Don't ask," I say, trudging up the stairs to get changed.

April I vommed.

Scream! It's hard work!!! So is the dream dead? Or does ACCOUNTABILITY mean you want me to say DOESN'T MATTER THAT YOU VOMMED—GET BACK OUT THERE, MY SON.

Yeah that. The second one.

I believe in you, vom or no vom.

CHAPTER 7

When I go back downstairs in my pajamas, my PE kit returned to its blue nylon bag at the back of my wardrobe, Mum is sitting on the sofa watching *First Dates* with a little production line of flat boxes and cookies wrapped in chic paper and ribbons and Post-it notes filled with addresses.

"Do you want me to help?" I ask.

"If you're not busy with whatever mysterious little scheme you're up to," she says, moving the pile of boxes from the sofa so I can sit down next to her.

"Never too busy to help my mummy," I say.

"Aaah, I see. This is about wanting Jake's room." She grins.

"No way! Firstly, how dare you?" I say. "And secondly . . . also how dare you?"

"I've known you since before you were born," she says, shaking her head. "You can't get anything past me."

"So what do you need me to do?"

"I need you to"—she looks around to find all the necessary equipment—"*neatly* write people's addresses on the boxes before you fold them into boxes, then you fold them, then you hand them to me, and I'll put the orders in the boxes. Got it?"

She turns the laptop toward me so I can see all her orders.

I nod. "Got it."

We sit in silence for a moment as I diligently copy out the first address from the screen onto the box before folding it and giving it to her.

"Like that?" I ask.

"Perfect," she says. "Such neat handwriting. You get that from your dad."

I smile. "Better that than his ears."

"Ha!" she says, but it rings a little hollow.

"So . . ." I say, wanting to turn the conversation away from my dad, "did you take those brownies next door?"

"I did," she says, stiffening a little in her seat. "It's funny, I wouldn't have recognized him at all if you hadn't mentioned it, but as soon as Ollie opened the door, I could totally see him as a little kid. He used to suck his thumb constantly; that's what I remember."

I smile. "You're right! I had forgotten that." He's clearly had braces, judging by that smile.

"I didn't see his mum. I think I do remember her . . . Italian lady, yeah? But I didn't think much of the dad, though."

"Oh?"

She shakes her head. "No, that's not fair of me. I'm sure he's perfectly nice. But he just rubbed me the wrong way a bit."

"How so?"

She sighs. "It just felt like he was very *keen* to make sure I understood that it wasn't his first choice to live here. Kept asking me questions about the estate across the road like it erupts into chaos every night as soon as the sun goes down."

"Yikes," I say.

"And you know, I just wanted to say to him: I've lived here for two decades, I chose to bring up my family here, and there's nothing wrong with it! I don't know . . . maybe I'm being sensitive. It just felt a bit rude, that's all."

"Not so rude you withheld your famous brownies, though."

"As if I could take them back!"

I shrug. "It would be one way to make an impression on the new neighbors."

"Apparently your little mate is going to Dawson for sixth form."

I frown, but I feel a flutter of excitement in my stomach at the thought of him being at my school. "I thought he went to St. Alfred's?"

"Well, it seems they've all gone down in the world," she says, raising her eyebrows.

"Ha!"

"Did you hear that?" Mum says, nodding at the TV. "They always say the same bloody thing on this program. That man with the tattoos just said he's *really family-oriented,* and the woman said, *Oooh yeah, me too. I'm really family-oriented.* Don't you think just for once it would be funny if someone said, *Oh, not me. I hate family. Can't stand it. Wouldn't save mine from a burning building?*"

I laugh. "Is that what you would say about us?"

"No, you silly sausage. I'd do anything for you lot."

"Even Jake?"

"Even him."

"Huh," I say as I try to remember where the *z* goes in Katarzyna. "You've got an order for April's mum!"

"I always tell her she doesn't have to pay full price, but she insists."

"That's what friends are for! If they're not willing to support you, who is?"

"You're so wise," Mum says as she strokes my hair.

In what feels like no time at all but is actually two solid hours of work, we've got all her orders ready for local delivery tomorrow.

She squeezes me tight before I head up to bed. "You are so good and so helpful and I love you so much." She releases me and goes to pick up her handbag and extract her purse. She hands me £30.

"I'm never one to turn down money, but you know you don't have to pay me to do this stuff."

"Just take it." She thrusts it at me.

"All right . . . if you insist. Remember, I'll help you any time you need me to. I know there's loads to get done."

"I just hate asking you lot to help me . . . I should be able to do it on my own—it's my business, after all! It's Bobbie's Bakery, not bloody . . . Sasha and Jake and Ruby and Bobbie's Bakery!"

"Yeah, but you just lost your local delivery driver . . ." I say quietly, still not used to the James being left off a list of Morgan family members. "So you're going to need help with something, somewhere."

"Ooooh, don't remind me," she says, grimacing. "Can you or Jake secretly drive?"

"No, but you could try Sasha."

"I could send Sasha out on her little pink bike and put a trailer on the back. Or would that be child labor?"

"Er, yes, I don't think a ten-year-old can work as a delivery driver, and I would miss you when you went to prison."

"You're very thoughtful." Mum squeezes me again. "I don't know what I'd do without you."

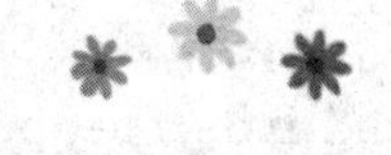

CHAPTER 8

The next day I decide to put Ollie's offer of help to the test.

My heart is beating furiously in my chest as I press the doorbell. It's like waiting outside my own house, except the wood paneling on the upstairs is painted green and ours is painted blue. I wait a few seconds and then decide it's a stupid idea, so I turn around to go, before realizing the front lawn gives me nowhere to escape to. As I'm scouting the terrain for a big plant to hide behind and cursing the fact that I am not a tiny little slip of a thing and able to crouch behind a rose bush, the door opens. I whip around and am faced by Ollie's dad. He smiles at me inquisitively with kind and soft brown eyes like Ollie's. Behind him, brown moving boxes are piled haphazardly in the hall, waiting to be broken down and recycled.

"Hello?"

"Oh, hello," I say, hoping I'm not looking too sweaty. "Is . . . Ollie there, please?"

"I think he's in his room. Let me just go and get him . . . one second. Who should I tell him is here?"

"Uh, Ruby. From last night," I say before wondering if that

sounds a bit suggestive and garbling. "I mean, last night, when he was running. And I was running. And then I was sick. He'll know who you mean."

Ollie's dad looks at me, bemused. "I'm sure he will . . ." He leaves the door ajar and I sit on the low wall that divides my front garden from his, already deep in regret. This is a stupid idea. Why would he want to help me? Why would he want to spend any time with me? He doesn't even know me! I probably only thought this was a good idea because I fancy him, which is *extremely* cringe.

When Ollie appears, he's even cuter than I remember. My regret deepens. He seems surprised I'm there. Ah, this is all so mortifying! I should have just abandoned this whole plan when I had the chance; now I'm in too deep, and for some reason getting my crush involved? Yikes.

"Hi," he says slowly, curiously.

"Hi," I say confidently, trying to dispel my embarrassment. I need help and I'm asking for help. That's it! "So. Regarding the running situation. Well, you know how Dawson borrows your school's—I mean, your *old* school's playing fields just before the start of term? That's for this race called the Dawson Dash."

"Yeah, I know about it. They even told me I could sign up when I came for my induction day. Seems like something they're very keen on . . . I might get involved. Why?"

"OK, right, well, I've decided I'm going to enter this year, which probably sounds really stupid because, come on, I'm not really an athlete, but anyway, I'm doing it. But I need some help, and I was wondering if maybe you could give me a hand?"

"Like . . . be your running coach?" he says, amused but with a warmth that surprises me.

Look at that cute smile! Ugh!

"I guess so," I say, shrugging and trying not to smile myself.

"You know I'm not an expert, right? I'm just some guy. I just want to manage your expectations . . ."

We've been standing there long enough that I breathe in his scent. The nostalgia it generates in me is powerful. Clean clothes. Freshly washed. Powdery. Pure comfort.

"Yeah, I'm not expecting, like, marathon training. I'm not entering the Olympics. I just need someone giving me a bit of structure, you know? And focus? Also I threw up the first time I went for a run, so . . ."

He grimaces. "I remember it well."

"I'd rather you didn't." We stand in silence for a moment. "So are you, like, up for it?"

"Sure." He shrugs. "Why not? It's not like I've got anything else to do this summer. Would be a good excuse to get me out of the house as well. I can't listen to another conversation about what specific shade of light blue to paint the bathroom."

"I honestly can't tell you how much I would appreciate it," I say. "I'll have to figure out a way to repay you."

"There's actually . . ." he starts before letting the thought drop off. "There's actually something I was hoping you could help me with."

"Oh?"

Now, that's a surprise. What could I possibly have to offer him?

"Yeah, um." He looks back over his shoulder before closing the front door. Intriguing! "So I want to start my own baking business. And I know that's what your mum does. She dropped off those brownies the other day, and it had her business card in the box. So I know it's not, like, a hobby for her."

"It most certainly isn't," I say, more gravely than I mean to. Possibly because of his intense vibes about not wanting to be overheard.

"So, yeah . . . I guess . . . it would be really helpful for me if I could ask her some questions sometime about how it all works, like . . . scaling up to making enough to sell, the logistics of it, what you need in place before you can sell stuff, you know?"

"Oh! Sure. I bet she would be happy to talk to you about that. She's a bit all over the place at the moment, since my dad moved out, but I'm sure she can tell you how to get started."

"Shit, sorry about your dad . . ." He frowns.

I shrug. "What can you do?"

"So do you want to get started soon, then?" Ollie thinks for a moment, doing some mental maths. "We've got, like, just over six weeks before the race. That's totally manageable."

It doesn't sound that manageable based on where I started off last night. It sounds very *un*manageable, in fact. But if Ollie thinks it can be done, who am I to argue?

"Yeah, the sooner, the better."

"Tomorrow?"

"Tomorrow is fine with me." I shrug again, a mix of nervousness about running and excitement about getting to spend more time with him. "Probably not . . . straight after a meal."

His face lights up. "Ha! OK, there will be no street vomiting on my watch. How about, like, five thirty tomorrow?"

"That sounds perfect," I say, nodding resolutely.

"It's weird. I already feel like this could actually be good fun!" Ollie's infused with a newfound enthusiasm.

I smile weakly. "Yeah . . ." I'm not convinced. "So I'll see you tomorrow. Out here at five thirty?"

"It's a deal. And let me know about your mum," he says, his hand on the door so he can get back in.

"I will!" I say before hopping over the wall back to my own front door.

"One more thing!" He sticks his head out of his door and catches me before I push mine open. "I saw the trainers you were wearing. You're going to absolutely kill your knees and ankles if you keep wearing those. I know it's not cheap, but you really have to wear proper trainers. It's not going to work without them, because you'll break your ankle next week, and then where will we be? Can't Dawson Dash on crutches!" He smiles widely. "Well, I guess you could . . . or at least you *should* be able to. But either way, better get some good trainers."

"OK, I'll try to figure that out before . . ." I think. "Well, before tomorrow evening!"

"See you then."

So that's that. I'll acquire some non-perilous trainers and a sports bra, and then I'll be heading out for my first session with Ollie. It's all sorted! My path to success is assured! "Ruby Morgan: star athlete" is on the horizon.

CHAPTER 9

"Are these too ugly, do you think?" I ask April.

She looks up from her phone. "I mean . . . they are *quite* gross. But all the running trainers I see before me"—she gestures around the discount sports shop—"are pretty horrible. And they're not the *literal* ugliest."

I sigh and walk around the shop floor a bit in the trainers, then pick up the box to check the price again. Based on that alone, and the fact that they fit, and the fact that uglier trainers exist, *and* the fact that they're not my plimsolls, they're a winner.

"Hey," I say. "Maybe the fact that they're ugly will count in my favor. If Ollie told me I had to get new trainers because mine were a death trap, he might take me more seriously in these chunky little monsters."

"Look at this," she says, holding her phone up to me. "How is she so talented?"

I sit down next to her on the bench in the trainer section and peer at her screen, seeing it's a video of Salma creating the most perfectly blended eye makeup to re-create a tropical sunset. Incredible.

"Ugh! Salma! Can you imagine being able to do that with eye shadow? Her mind!"

"Not even just her mind! Her steady hands! She's so talented it makes me scream!"

"Same," I say, while wondering if I have the mental strength to even try looking for a sports bra in here. Unfortunately I do *need* one, as a few seconds of bouncing the other night proved to me. On the balance of things, breaking my jaw with my own boobs seems like a greater danger than trying to buy something in a shop and finding they don't have my size, which, as a longtime fat girl, is something I'm already *very* used to.

I go hunting through a rack of sports bras for anything that might fit. No luck. Jesus, it's like they don't *want* chunky babes like me to be working out. What's that about? Nothing is even close! I actually get down on the floor and make sure there isn't something lurking down the back of the rack. Nope.

"This is so bullshit!" I fume at April. "I knew something like this was going to happen. Before I've even properly gotten started as well!"

"It's *extremely* bullshit," she agrees. "But I will not let you be deterred! Let's explore the clearance rack." She steers me in the direction of the row of items with red stickers, and methodically we go through each bra, checking the labels just in case.

"Aha!" cries April, thrusting a neon-pink-and-silver Lycra monstrosity in my face.

"Thanks, I hate it," I say. "But I understand and I accept that I have no choice." I close my eyes and cross myself like I'm entering a church. I even double-check the size label to make sure. Yep, it's right. Between this and the trainers, I now consider myself fully equipped for my challenge.

Maybe it's the inability to find more than one single solitary item in my size, but as I move through the sports shop to get to the till, I feel a prickle of self-consciousness. Like I don't belong here, like I'm out of place. I wonder if people are looking at me and thinking the same thing, wondering what I'm doing here or, even worse, thinking, *Oooh, good for her*. But they're probably not thinking about me at all. They're just getting on with whatever they're there for.

"I'll pay for these and then we can head home. Thank you for accompanying me on my epic quest."

"There is simply no one I would rather loiter with than you," she says.

The dude behind the counter doesn't interrogate me on the reasons for my purchase or ensure I'm somehow qualified to own trainers. He just lets me pay for them and go.

"I do wish lower Sydenham and actual Sydenham weren't separated by a big hill," I say, doing my most determined stomp back up Perry Rise.

"Consider it race training," April says, nudging me with her hip.

"You're not tempted to enter?" I ask. "Keep your old pal Ruby company?"

"Ha!" She barks a loud laugh. "Oh, wait, are you serious?"

I shrug. "If I can do it!" I say brightly, then add, "Which, let's face it, I'm not sure I can."

"Since when have I been *inspired* by organized sports of any kind?"

"Since never," I concede. Clearly I'm not going to be able to rope April into this one.

"And anyway, you don't need company! You've got Ollie Cowan now!"

I feel a bit sick at the mention of his name. "I guess . . ." I think for a moment. "Do you *really* not remember anything interesting about him from Scouts? I'm just trying to gather as much information as possible about him to inform whether he's an appropriate crush."

April shrugs. "He was pretty quiet, but, like . . . nice, not a horrible *boy* kind of boy, you know?"

There's not a lot to work with there. I guess I'll just have to find out for myself. But every time I have some thought about getting to know Ollie, I immediately feel discouraged, embarrassed, ashamed, like if he knew I thought he was cute, he wouldn't want to help me in the way he agreed to.

"How often are you going to be running with him?" April asks once we've made it to the top of Perry Rise. Chatter and the clinking of glasses floats out of the pub beer garden on the corner of the little alley down to where April lives. It has a big cowboy boot on the roof for reasons no one fully understands. This is southeast London, not the Wild West.

"I don't know. I hadn't actually thought about it . . ."

"It's *quite* a commitment, starting from, well, no offense, but starting from nothing."

"How dare you! I am an athlete!" I say, flicking her arm. "But seriously, yeah, I don't actually know. It's, like, six weeks away from now, so I probably need to, horror of horrors, make a bit of an effort."

"I believe in you!" April says, uncharacteristically cheerily as she hugs me goodbye outside her front door. "Let me know how it goes! I'm invested! But, er, don't go at it too hard. I think if I get another text about you vomming, then I'll have to physically restrain you from going any further with this escapade."

"You really think I can do this?" I ask. Surely I can't vom again.

"I think you are a beautiful and powerful beast and that you can do anything you put your mind to."

"I appreciate your optimism."

I walk the rest of the way home alone. I may be practically equipped, but am I mentally prepared?

CHAPTER 10

When I get home, Mum is sitting on the living room floor, photos spread around her on the carpet. Uh-oh, this doesn't look good.

"What are you up to?" I ask her, dumping the shopping bag on the stairs.

"I was looking for this roll of pink ribbon to wrap order boxes in. I was sure it was in one of the boxes in the living room, but instead I found these cute pictures of us all at Disney . . . I thought I would send one to your dad. I bet he doesn't have any physical photos of you lot."

I pick up one from the pile next to her. Jake, Sasha, and me at Disneyland Paris when we were mostly there for Sasha's benefit and Jake and I were definitely too old for it but still had the best time. "Ugh! Twelve was *such* an un-cute age for me," I say, balking at the too-thin eyebrows. Why was I messing with my eyebrows?! Thank God they grew back all right.

"No way! You've always been a little cutie," she says, handing over one of Jake and me on a blustery-looking British beach at six and four, before Sasha even existed. To be fair, I do look extremely cute in that one.

Thud, thud, thud we hear from the floor above. Jake stomping this way.

"Jesus!" Jake shouts from the stairs. "Are you trying to kill me, leaving this lying around on the stairs to trip over?" I hear him kick the bag with my shiny new trainers and hard-won sports bra inside.

"Don't you have eyes?" I ask him impatiently as he bursts in, equally impatiently.

"That's not the point. What are you doing anyway?" He sits down on the arm of the sofa next to me. Couldn't sit *on* the sofa—has to signal how busy and important he is by sitting on the *arm* of the sofa.

"Looking at photos," I say, handing him the two that Mum gave me. "Getting some together for Dad." The idea that Dad needs photos of us because he doesn't see us every day is truly weird and horrible and something I don't know if I'll ever get used to.

"God," Jake says, throwing the Disneyland photo back to Mum on the floor. "Don't send him *that* one. Look how fat I was. Gross."

Oh yes, didn't I mention? The reason Jake thinks he can be such a dick to me about my body is because he's a Former Fat Person. In many cases a Former Fat Person is a more dangerous entity than an always-thin person, which is *definitely* true for Jake. He did it, so why can't I?! Maybe because I don't want to, shithead! Maybe because I don't think it's the be-all and end-all! Ever thought of that, huh? No, of course he hasn't.

I sigh. "You look fine."

"You would say that," he says dismissively, jumping back to his feet.

"I would say it because it's true. Do you know how painful it is for me to not tell you that you look like pure molten garbage?" I lob at him before he manages to leave the room.

"Stop it, you two," Mum says with such exasperation that we do.

Here's the thing: Jake and I clearly feel differently about our bodies. That's fine. But I don't get why he's decided his way is the One True Way! Just let me live my life, you know?

I leave Mum in the living room, sorting out the photos, and drag myself and my shopping bag upstairs. I flop on the bed and read half of *Fun Home* by Alison Bechdel again, because my brain is all full and buzzy and annoying, so I need something that's familiar and comforting that I don't have to focus on too hard. I honestly just need Jake to leave me alone. Let me chub in peace. I don't need to hear some nonsense every day of my life about how inadequate my body is and how superior he is to me now. How can you be superior if you're going around trying to make everyone feel stressed out about the way they look, hmmm? Riddle me that! Good thing I have the mental fortitude of an ox (*and the body of one, hurr hurr,* says the Jake in my brain) and can just get on with my life in spite of his nonsense.

At five twenty-five, I put on my new sports bra, a T-shirt, leggings, socks, and my new trainers. I look at myself in the mirror. I'm nervous and very conscious of how far out of my comfort zone I'm going to be. But that's not a reason to chicken out now.

Is this what a runner looks like? Hell yes. Hell yes, it is!

CHAPTER 11

"You're on time!" Ollie says, smiling, as I emerge from my front door. He's wearing those very short shorts again.

"Of course! This is important!" *Don't stare at his thighs. Don't stare at his thighs. Don't stare at his thighs.*

He looks down at my feet. "They look *loads* better."

"Oh good. I wasn't sure what to buy, but . . . uh, they were cheap, so . . ."

"Not a bad place to start, and if you find you like running, you can always upgrade later."

"This is strictly an eyes-on-the-prize scenario," I tell him as we walk to the end of the road with the footbridge across the railway line. "I'm doing this for the Dawson Dash. For spite purposes. End of story."

He looks at me curiously but just nods. "OK, got it. Eyes on the prize."

"So . . ." I say. "Where are we going? And why are we walking?"

"We're going to the park. And we're walking because . . . it's a warm-up."

"Oh yeah, of course. Can't be running everywhere, all the time."

"No, exactly," he says, smiling kindly. "We don't need you running the second you come out the door, before your legs even know what's going on." We climb the steps up to the bridge. Oooh, already a little out of breath! Great start!

"Got it." Maybe that was my first mistake on the Night of Vom.

"So . . . the Dawson Dash," he says.

I'm slowly edging down the steps on the other side of the railway bridge, which are so steep that they've always struck me as the place I'm likely to meet my peril.

"Yep. I need to win it."

He stops dead in front of me and turns to look at me over his shoulder. "Win it?"

"Yeah," I say nonchalantly.

"OK," he says. "This will be more of a challenge than I was expecting, but I can roll with it."

I jump down from the last step. "I'm dreaming big!"

"You've *got* to dream big," he says, and when he smiles, a little dimple is carved out on each of his cheeks and it makes me want to scream.

When we get to Mayow Park, it's still full of families and little sports teams and joggers. I suppose that's what we are too now! I never thought I would see the day.

"OK," says Ollie, looking up from his phone. "Are you ready?"

I swallow nervously. This is it! "Yeah . . . I'm ready."

"Let's go!"

Oh! He's actually running off ahead of me! When he said *Let's go*, he actually meant it! Better get going, then . . . I jog after him and find he's not actually going that fast at all. This is manageable! It's even, dare I say it . . . a little slow?

"Stop!" he says when an alarm beeps on his phone, and he slows down to walking.

"What, now?" I ask almost indignantly. It was only just getting hard!

"Yes, now!"

I slow to a walk to match his pace. A huge Bernese mountain dog passes us, plodding down the path with its thick tree-trunk legs.

"Now we'll walk for a bit," he says, setting another alarm.

"OK . . ." I say.

"And then we're going to do all this another six times."

"Huh," I say, glad that he seems to have some sort of plan.

As we walk, I wonder if it's OK to chat to him or if this is a strictly business situation. "So," I venture finally, "what subjects are you going to do when you start at Dawson?"

"Uh, maths—" The alarm goes off again. "Time to run!"

And with that, he picks up his heels and starts to jog. If I just have to do what I did before, then that's fine with me. I run after him until the countdown goes off and it's back to walking.

"Where were we?" he says. "Oh yes. I'm going to be doing maths, chemistry, geography, and art, just to keep things spicy."

"My best friend, April, is an absolute freak for maths. Look out for her—she'll be the skinny little goth."

"Good to know. But you don't do maths, right?"

"No way. Very much *not* my shit."

"And what is your shit?"

"My future shit is history, politics, Spanish, and English."

"Nice." He nods approvingly. Maybe it's having that very basic and long-ago foundation of having known each other before, but he has such an easy way about him. I don't know what I was expecting. Maybe someone . . . edgier? Meaner? I don't know. My brain's probably been ruined by all the other horrible boys at school. My expectations of cute guys are not high!

We're interrupted by the phone beeping. "Let's go!"

This time it's a little harder. My earlier triumph, the thought that I could have kept going beyond the end of the timer, is starting to feel like a distant memory by the end of this run. My lungs are tight, and when Ollie announces it's time to slow down, my breathing is fast and doesn't return to normal straightaway.

"Getting harder, huh?" he says. "I told you: I have a plan!"

"So I see," I say, embarrassed by how little it's taken to get me panting.

He takes the hint and doesn't pick up the conversation again this time, instead letting me regain my breath. Which is nice of him. Except by the time the next run comes around, I haven't actually gotten my breath back. This is just getting harder and harder! I thought I was doing so well with the first run!

By the time we get to the last run, I'm properly finished. My calves are burning and I can hardly speak. But it's over.

Ollie claps me on the shoulder. "You did it! Your first run finished!"

"It doesn't really count, though, does it?"

"Why not?"

"It was mostly walking . . ." I say, panting from the effort.

"It counts!"

"If you insist . . ."

I look at my phone as we're heading out of the park on the way home. It's only just after six o'clock! Including the walk there, we can't have been in the park for more than twenty minutes! I thought he understood that time was very much of the essence on Operation Star Athlete! I mean, not that I would have been able to do much more than I did today anyway. This doesn't bode well for the aforementioned Operation Star Athlete, does it?

I'm about to say something to that effect when Ollie says, "I like Mayow Park, but let's mix it up. It's good not to get stuck doing the same route all the time."

"Variety is the spice of life," I say, raising my eyebrows at him suggestively, although I'm not sure *what* I'm suggesting. And right now I must look like a tomato with eyebrows.

"I couldn't agree more. Ugh, these steps are a killer," he says as we head back over the railway bridge.

"I didn't think fit people even noticed that," I say, very sure of the fact that I will forever be an Unfit Person.

"Ha! You're funny," he says.

I wasn't even trying to be funny.

"So . . . are you, like"—I put my fingers up in air quotes—"'sporty'?"

He smiles again. "I guess so? I was on the rugby team at my old school and played hockey as well. And I like running."

"Well, I'm glad you like running because otherwise I would feel bad about dragging you out just to assist me in my little quest."

"I would be out running anyway. This just means I'm doing it a little bit differently than usual." He shrugs like it's nothing major when I'm clearly holding him back from his well-established schedule.

"Well . . . I really appreciate it."

"Don't thank me yet! This is just the beginning!"

I see the screen of my phone illuminate. It's a call from Dad. I just stare at the screen for a few seconds. I'll call him back later. Or should I pick up now and tell him I'll call back later? I'll just call him back later. But talking to him is still so weird that I don't know if I actually *want* to call him back later. And then I realize I've been silent for too long and Ollie is waiting for me to say something.

"I'm up for the challenge," I say quickly. "I've got to see this through. It's a matter of principle."

"*Principle*, is it?"

"Yep! What can I say, I'm a principled kinda gal!" Where did that come from?

"Well." We've arrived back at my house. "No point overdoing it, so let's not go out again tomorrow, but is the day after OK?"

I think about it for a second. "Yeah, that's fine with me," I say, shrugging.

"See you then. Same time, same place."

"See you then!" I say, slipping my key into the door. "And thanks!"

Extremely unfortunately for me, on the other side of the door is Jake, coming down the stairs. He takes one look at my pink face and matted hair and leggings.

"Oh my God!" He bursts into laughter. "You're really? You're actually?" It's like he literally cannot comprehend it.

"Mmm-hmmm," I say. "You'd better believe it."

"What?" shouts Mum from the living room.

"Nothing!" I shout back.

"Ruby's been for a run!" Jake calls to her.

"Oh!" she says, surprised.

I walk in to see her. "Jake was being a dickhead, so I, once again, took things too far and told him I could win the Dawson Dash if I wanted to, and now I'm training."

"Good for you," says Mum. Jake's sloped in to join us.

"I've just had a thought," I say. "If I win, can I have your bedroom?"

Jake laughs. "Er, yeah, you can have my bedroom and you can have my first student loan installment of next term as well."

I hold out my hand to shake his.

"You're serious?" he asks.

"I'm serious. The question is, Are you?"

He furrows his brow. "All right, then." He grips my hand like I'm a walnut and he's a nutcracker and stalks into the kitchen. Do they teach brutal handshakes at Oxford?

Mum sighs, long used to refereeing between Jake and me. "As long as you two sort it out between yourselves, I don't care how you do it."

When I'm sitting on my bed post-shower with a hairdryer pointed directly at my thick hair, all I can think is *I need to call Dad back.* But I don't. And I don't call him back before dinner. Or after dinner. Or before bed. I'll do it in the morning. Won't I?

CHAPTER 12

In the end, I don't call him back, but I do text him. Calling him just feels too weird. Having to tell him about my day because he's not there to talk to in person? Weird. Decidedly weird. Texting feels slightly more normal, but I know I won't be able to avoid properly speaking to him sometime soon. His texts are cheery, but so are mine, I guess. I don't tell him about running. I mean, I've only gone once so there isn't much to tell. I suppose what I mean is that I don't tell him that I'm entering the Dawson Dash. It would feel too awkward—maybe because I don't want to have to go over *why* I'm doing it (because Jake is a dick, because Jake thinks I can't do it, because I want to prove to Sasha that she doesn't have to let other people limit her beliefs). Those reasons feel private to me.

Two days after my first meeting with Ollie, I'm back at it again. When I leave my house that evening, I half expect Ollie not to be there. But there he is in those micro blue shorts and a T-shirt with a hole in the hem.

"You came back!" he says.

"I was thinking the same thing about you," I say, smiling.

"Why wouldn't I?"

"Because it's tedious." I sigh.

"No way. It's a fun challenge for me. I've never done something like this before!"

"Why would you? Most people can just sort of . . . do it. No help required."

He shakes his head. "Nah, everyone's different. And it's good to ask for help sometimes."

Personally I'm not a fan, but I don't tell him that.

We set off in the opposite direction, and Ollie clearly has a destination in mind.

"Where to today?" I ask him.

"Wells Park," he says, which immediately strikes fear into my heart.

"I hate to break it to you," I say, "but Wells Park is on a hill."

"Yeeeees?" he says, looking at me sideways.

"Do I look like I can run up a hill?"

"You look like you can do anything you want, but since we're only doing short bursts, we can always have you run down the slopes, then walk back up in your rest period," he says, shrugging.

"OK, I like the sound of that. Or at least I don't hate the sound of that."

"Good! Because you're not meant to hate this, you know?"

"What do you mean?"

"Like . . . this is completely optional . . . so if you really hate it, you don't have to do it, right?"

I blush, feeling a little stupid. "No, I know that. But the same goes for you."

He holds up his hands defensively. "This is fun for me! But if you're going to dread it every time we go out, then . . ."

I clear my throat decisively. "No, it's fine. I don't dread it. I'm looking forward to giving it another go." That's a lie, but he doesn't seem to notice.

When we get to Wells Park, two guys are playing table tennis on the public table on the corner. Why couldn't the Dawson Dash be a table-tennis tournament instead of a five-kilometer run? Now, that's a sport I can get behind. We walk to the top of the park and then set off.

"Let's go!" he says, and I trot along just behind him. True to his word, we go down the hill. "Stop!"

I slow to a walk. "That wasn't very long," I say, a mixture of surprised and grateful.

"It's the same as we did the other day," he says, turning us back around and heading up the slope again.

"Oh . . ." I say. I guess I thought we would be making progress, rather than repeating the same thing.

"That's how this is going to work! Repetition until you find it easy enough to move on!"

"Got it," I say.

We've barely made it back to the top when it's time to run again, and, once again, it feels almost *too* easy.

Ollie senses it too. "OK, no more running downhill for you." He gestures upward. "There's a path that cuts through the middle of the park, so we'll stick to that. It's a compromise."

I sigh theatrically. "I suppose."

And, yes, running on the flat ground rather than down the hill is a little more challenging, but by the end of the session, I'm surprised to find that I'm not panting *quite* so much as I was at the end of the first. Huh! Maybe he's onto something!

"You feeling good?" he asks as we slow down to a walk after the last run.

"Ish," I say. I still feel stupid about how unfit I am in front of him. He doesn't even break a sweat doing what we're doing! I just can't imagine ever being at that level, like running is natural rather than something my body is shocked and appalled by.

"You should bring water with you," he says. "Your body needs water. Everyone's body needs water! Plus it's something to do with your hands while you run."

"I was wondering about that," I say. "It felt excessive to be, like . . . aggressively pumping my arms like I'm in the Olympics or something. But if I didn't do anything, I thought it probably looked weird."

"I like the combination of water in one hand and phone in the other. But you don't need to be holding your phone, so water will have to do!"

"Got it." He's right. I don't want to dehydrate like a raisin in the sun. Gotta keep this skin hydrated and bouncy like a little peach. Also I guess it must be good for my internal organs.

We head out of the park and down toward the main road, through the estate that's built on either side of the street.

"Ruby!" I hear someone call, and I know without even looking up that it's Jessica.

"Hey!" I wave back.

She's leaning over the wall of the walkway out the front of their first-floor flat, eating a blue Popsicle.

"What are you up to?" she shouts.

"Running, of course!" I shout back.

"Of course! Who's your friend?"

"This is Ollie," I say, reddening, although you probably wouldn't be able to tell under my pink sweaty-face situation.

"Hi, Ollie!" She waves.

He squints up at her and waves back.

"Well, I'll text you," I say.

"You'd better," she shouts.

We continue our walk home, but seeing Jessica while I'm out with Ollie has poked at that little insecure place inside me. Like, *Oh, that's what a pretty girl looks like*. Like, *Oh, how mortifying to fancy someone who wouldn't look twice at me.*

"Friend of yours?" he says, smiling, interrupting the thought and bringing me back to the moment.

"One of my best friends, Jessica." Now, she's probably the kind of girl Ollie wants. Pretty, relaxed. And, crucially, thin. Wanting to change the subject, I say, "Are any of your friends coming to Dawson?"

He clears his throat and looks around at the street, like he's concentrating very intently. "Uh, no, I don't think so."

It must be weird moving to somewhere as big and chaotic as Dawson. I've been there since I was eleven, so I'm used to it, but it can't be easy for the people who join for sixth form. "Well, you'll meet enough people on day one, so I wouldn't worry about it."

I go home and shower, and by the time I come out, the group chat is already aflame.

Jessica: Ruby got a man and didn't tell anyone

Salma: Oh my days who

Jessica: Ginger boy. Tall and skinny one

Salma: Idk

April: Ollie Cowan, blast from her past, p sure he's not her man . . . yet

Jessica: What's all this about

April: Dawson Dash isn't it

Salma: Is it!

Jessica: Sick! So you're my competition now Ruby

Salma: You running it, April or nah? I can't decide

April: It's a no from me dawg but you do you

Ruby: HELLO I AM HERE no he is not my man yes I am doing Dawson Dash please keep me accountable don't let me flake I have to do this to show my dickhead brother who's boss

Salma: Your fit brother

Ruby: Gross

Jessica: Why are you booing her she's right

Ruby: Gross

When I'm pulling out some clothes to wear at dinner, I think of Sasha on the sofa the other day, asking if her arms were "too squishy." I yank a white vest out of my drawer and put it on. I've still got insecurities of my own, but I still want to do what I can for hers.

CHAPTER 13

By the time we do our same little routine for a third time, I feel, dare I say it, like I've actually made some progress. Not as much as I would like, but, to be honest, my standards are so high that I would ideally like to be able to run the race by now—even though we're only one week in. Progress nonetheless. Is it easy? No. But do I feel different after doing it for a third time than I felt after doing it for the first time? Yes.

I'm almost a bit sad when it's the weekend and I have two days off in a row, but Monday comes around again quickly enough.

"Crystal Palace Park OK with you?" Ollie asks when we convene outside our front doors on Monday evening.

"Fine with me," I tell him. "I can be one of the joggers I look at while I'm skating and thinking, *How are they doing that? And more importantly . . . why?*"

He laughs. "Do you skateboard? That's cool."

"No, I'm in a little roller-skating crew with my three best friends. April—the goth one from your future maths class; Jessica, who you met the other day; and my friend Salma. She's, like, a science genius but also a makeup genius. Oh, and a video genius too—her transitions are insane. Hey, Crystal Palace is another one with tons of hills!" I exclaim, realizing I have been played.

"I'll find us a nice flat bit."

"Promise?" I ask.

"Promise," he says, rolling his eyes.

"I'm sorry! I just have needs!"

"I see that," he says, smiling.

I wonder what it would have been like if we'd gone to the same primary school and then he'd gone to Dawson and we'd known each other the whole time. I wonder if we'd be friends now. I wonder if I would even fancy him or if the friendship would have neutralized that a bit. Who knows, maybe we wouldn't be friends at all.

"Hey," I say, seizing the moment since the walk to Crystal Palace Park is a bit longer. "How come you moved house? And how come you're coming to Dawson for sixth form?"

He sighs. And then he swallows. "Well," he says. "It's all part of the same thing really."

"Yeah?"

"So my parents had this restaurant. I don't know if you remember her at all from when we were at nursery school, but my mum's Italian, and she and my dad had this Italian restaurant. In Crystal Palace. It was called Zanetti's—that was her maiden name. Anyway, it was really popular, really successful, brought in loads of money and all that."

"Yeah," I say, nodding. I sense a fall is coming.

"So they opened a second restaurant in Dulwich. And that was sort of the beginning of the end really. The first restaurant worked because my parents were able to keep an eye on everything, stay on top of everything, do quality control, all of that. And then splitting their attention between two locations was just too much, and then there was some stuff with their accountant that made it all worse, and it was like all at once people sort of stopped coming because the quality went downhill, *and* they had this big tax bill to pay." He shrugs. "And that was that. Both restaurants gone."

I don't want to interrupt him, but I can't stop myself from saying, "I'm sorry."

"So . . . I used to go to St. Alfred's," he says, looking at me out of the corner of his eye.

"Fancy," I say. St. Alfred's is definitely the fanciest school around here.

"Yeah, well, it's all a load of bollocks anyway," he says bitterly. "So I went to the prep school and I went to the secondary school, but obviously when the restaurant closed and there was, like . . . no more money, I wasn't going to be able to stay on for the sixth form. No great loss to me, though. But my parents had pumped basically all their money into keeping the business afloat, keeping people employed, even when it was clear it just wasn't working anymore. It was like they just couldn't give up the dream." I'm slightly surprised by how much he's talking. It makes me wonder if he doesn't usually have a place to put all these thoughts.

"So that's why you're at Dawson."

"Yeah," he says. "And then we had to move because my parents needed to . . . Well, they basically had to sell the house to clear their debts."

I think of my mum taking the brownies next door, how cagey his dad was about the neighborhood. "Where did you live before?"

"Dulwich," he says, sighing.

"Again, I say to you, *fancy*." I smile.

"If you like that sort of thing."

"You didn't?"

He shakes his head. "I never really felt like I belonged there. It was like my parents were always trying too hard to fit in, to have what everyone else had, instead of just, like, being happy? Being normal? And always trying to do more, have more—where did that even get them in the end?" A cloud comes over his face. I can tell he doesn't want to talk about it anymore.

"Thank you for filling in the gap," I say. "At least now I know what happened to you since I last saw you."

He nods. We walk the rest of the way to the park in silence, which makes me feel bad for asking. But how could I have known it was all so messy?

"Right," he says when we get there. "Let's get going on this one." It's like he wants to get it over and done with. I feel like I've poisoned the mood somehow.

"Yep. What are we doing this week?"

"Same as last week, just a bit longer."

"Right," I say. "I think I can do that."

When are we going to get to the good stuff? When I'm ready, I guess.

When Ollie said *just a bit longer*, what he actually meant was running for twice as long as last week. And, yes, in my case that was bursts of one single solitary minute, but doubling that up already feels like a challenge. Maybe I shouldn't be *quite* so keen to accelerate things.

"Let's get it done!" he says to me over his shoulder when it's clear I'm staggering my way through the last run of the day.

"I'll . . . try . . ." I pant, grateful that he doesn't attempt to engage me in conversation. This is, and I cannot stress this enough, the longest two minutes of my life so far. I feel like my lungs are going to collapse. How do people run for any longer than this?

"Stop!" Ollie says, and turns to me with a triumphant smile. "Now you know you've got it in you! And all you have to do is do that again on Wednesday!"

"What about Friday?" I ask between gasps.

"On Friday we'll try *three* minutes."

I nod resolutely. "I am going to choose to believe in myself."

"Damn right you are." He nudges me in the side with his elbow, which I can't say I altogether approve of. But at least maybe I didn't totally ruin everything by being my usual nosy self.

"Sorry for asking, like, intrusive questions earlier," I say on our walk home.

"It's OK," he says, shrugging his square shoulders loosely in that easy Ollie way. "It's been such a big part of my life for the past couple of years, I guess, that it's a bit impossible not to mention it at some point. It's got into everything." He swallows.

"Everything?" I ask.

"It *feels* like everything," he says.

I wonder if I could talk this freely to him about, like, my parents' separation. But it feels too new, and I don't really even know how to talk about it yet or what to say.

"That's why I was asking about your mum's bakery on the sly."

"Oh yeah," I say, furrowing my brow.

"So that's what I want to do. I mean, it's what I *do* do now. I love to bake, invent new recipes, try out things and refine them until I've got it right and it's the most perfect-tasting cake or cookie or blondie or whatever that I can imagine."

"Huh!" I say. I'm a little surprised, but I don't know why I should be. It's not like I know him after all.

"But my parents are so *scarred* by the whole ordeal that the last thing they want is for me to get into that line of work. They've practically forbidden it. Because I'm good at maths they've decided the logical progression is for me to get into *finance*." He curls his lip.

"How *can* they forbid you?"

"Well, I don't mean they've literally forbidden it, but every time I mention wanting to go to catering college and training to be a pastry chef or, horror of horrors, not going anywhere and just starting my own thing, they just sort of . . . laugh it off, like, of course I couldn't possibly mean that's what I want to do. I'm always trying new stuff out as practice, learning what I like to do, what I'm good at, but I always have to lie about why I'm making things. I say it's someone's birthday or I volunteered for a bake sale or something," he says, shielding his eyes from the sun as he looks at me. "So I end up giving the stuff I make to random people on the street after testing it because I don't know what else to do with it!"

"That's cute," I say, smiling.

"I'm just sick of humoring my parents about the whole thing . . . but now just feels like the worst time to try to make them understand it's what I want."

I feel like a butterfly has come and landed on my hand and I don't want to scare it off and make it fly away. I want to know all about Ollie, but I don't want to be *too* interested. "Do they think they're, like . . . protecting you?"

"I guess," he says. "But they're really just inhibiting me. I'm not going to go through what they went through, and even if I do, it's my decision."

"So they think you should go into finance instead?"

"Before they had the restaurant, my dad started out in finance, so obviously he's just like, *Oh yes, that's always a good idea, go do that, study economics at university*, and I'm like . . . I don't *want* to go to university. Which they can't get their heads around. Anyway." He looks embarrassed at how much he's shared. "I'm not used to talking about myself this much. I clearly don't know when to stop."

"No, no," I say, which of course I would because what could be more interesting to anyone (specifically me) than learning about the person they fancy (specifically Ollie)? "It's really fine. It's good to talk." And then a thought comes to me. "Hey . . . you know how you wanted to talk to my mum about her business?"

"Yeah," he says, looking keen.

"Do you have a bike?"

"Like just a bike? Like a normal bike?"

When I nod, he goes on.

"Yeah, it's a bit battered, but I like to get out every few week-ends. Why?"

"Well, for reasons I don't need to get into now, my mum recently lost her local delivery driver, and I get the distinct feeling it would enhance her life if she had someone trustworthy who could drive—or, I guess, cycle, why not?—around to Sydenham, Forest Hill, Dulwich, Crystal Palace, you know, the usual places, and drop off her orders."

"I would definitely be up for that!"

"I bet she would pay you decently as well," I say, thinking of my £30 in exchange for not much labor the other week. "I mean, it's not confirmed or anything, but I bet it would help her loads, so I can mention it to her if you're up for it?"

"Definitely!" He looks genuinely delighted.

"That way you could make a bit of money and have an excuse to ask her anything you want to know. And help her out too."

"Her brownies were amazing. I thought I was all brownie-d out in my life. Like, I never make them myself anymore, but hers are just perfect," he says reverently.

"So I'll ask my mum when I get home, yeah? She has this little trailer thing you can clip on the back of your bike, and she'd put the boxes in there."

"Yeah, that sounds great to me. But just one thing—don't mention it to my parents. It makes my life easier if they think I've abandoned the whole idea of baking, pastry chefing, all of that. If they knew I was trying to learn the ins and outs of running a business like that . . ."

"I hear you," I say, nodding.

I want to help him! He's helping me so much that I feel I should give him something in return.

"Mum!" I shout when I get home, slamming the door behind me triumphantly.

"What?!" she shouts back from the kitchen. "And don't slam the door! I'm all on edge doing this icing. One wrong move and I'll be in trouble."

"Sorry," I say, sheepishly slinking into the kitchen where she's meticulously piping a swirl of pink icing on top of a parade of cupcakes for a second birthday party. "But I've solved all your problems. Or at least one of them."

She puts down the icing bag and looks at me expectantly. "Well?"

"You know Ollie next door?"

"Your old-new best friend," she says, smiling. "Yes, I know who you mean."

"OK, well, he's really keen to get into baking. Like, as a *career*. He seems pretty dedicated and wants to do it properly once we finish school."

"I don't need an apprentice right now, Roo!" she says, eyes wide, like I've invited him into our home for eight hours a day.

"No, it's not that," I say, waving her away. "He's all outdoorsy and likes to cycle and has his own bike, so I was thinking maybe he could do your local deliveries?"

She looks thoughtful for a moment. "Wow . . . now that *would* actually solve some of my problems . . ."

"See? I'm not so useless after all! And you could pay him a bit, right?"

"Yes, of course. I'm not going to let some boy I barely know cycle around southeast London for me for hours for the good of his health."

"And maybe you could tell him some stuff about, like, hygiene certification from the council and starting out in markets and all of that?"

"I'd be happy to!" she says. "Do you think he could do it for me this weekend? I need to drop these cakes off at the birthday party myself, which is really messing with my plans."

"I don't know, but I can ask him," I say, shrugging. "Am I your favorite child?"

"You're my favorite child in this room," she says, narrowing her eyes at me.

"Hey!" Sasha pipes up from the living room before plodding into the kitchen. "What about now?"

Mum throws her hands up in defeat. "Well, you've got me there!"

"You all right, Sash?" I ask her.

She nods, her round cheeks bobbing up and down like cute little apples. "I just spoke to Dad. He says you should call him when you feel like it."

Mum clears her throat. "You should, Roo. Have a Zoom with him or something so you can see each other."

"Yeah, yeah, I will," I say, waving it off.

"He said you haven't called him in ages," Sasha says imploringly.

"I know I haven't," I say, a little impatient. Just a little. I don't like being pinned down like this!

"Why not?" she asks, because she doesn't know when to stop.

Mum just looks at us nervously.

"Because! Just because! Because I still find it weird to update him on my life because he doesn't know what I'm up to! And because I don't want to hear about *his* new life! So what's the point?"

"But it's Dad," Sasha says, sounding hurt on his behalf, which makes me want to cry.

"I know," I say, softening. "I'll call him."

I wake up that night to the sound of crying and sniffing coming from outside. This time I don't need to put my face to the window to know it's Mum.

CHAPTER 14

When I get home, all tired and happy-buzzy from a little skating session in the park with April and Salma and Jessica the next day, Ollie is in the living room. He looks up and greets me with one of those smiles. Ambushed in my own home? By the cutest boy I know? Who makes me feel sick with butterflies? Outrageous.

"Hey, Ruby," he says. "Thanks so much for sorting this!"

"I don't know if you'll be thanking her when you've done your first round," says Mum, grimacing. "If you really hate it, just tell me, and I'll pay you for this week and we'll never speak of it again."

"No, no, I promise I'll do a good job," he says eagerly.

"It's funny. I didn't think I remembered you from when you were little, but now that you're here, it's all coming back. You were such a *polite* little boy, never, you know, grabby or pushing. Always very quiet and waiting your turn. Which made it even funnier that you and Ruby wanted to play together all the time!"

"Are you saying I was grabby?"

She just looks at me and crosses her arms over her chest. "Anyway, Ollie, do you feel like you know what you're doing?"

He nods. "Yep, I've got all the addresses on my phone sorted by area. I've got my route. I've clipped the trailer to my bike. What could possibly go wrong?"

"Don't say that. It'll stress me out," says Mum.

"No more stress!" I say to her, clapping my hands decisively. "Ollie's on it. And all you have to do in exchange is give him money and share your trade secrets."

"If it leaves me more time to fulfill orders, then that's fine with me."

I help them put the boxes in the trailer in order of where he's going to be dropping them off, then wave to him as he cycles away.

"Nice boy," says Mum once he's disappeared around the corner to the main road.

"Yeah," I say flatly. No need for too much enthusiasm.

She looks at me out of the corner of her eye. "Oh, it's like that, is it?"

"Like what?"

"Nothing . . ." She grins.

"Ugh!"

"Ollie brought us some chocolate orange brownies with real orange zest on the top for me to see what I thought."

"Nice boy," I say quietly.

We go back inside and I shout to Sasha and her little mate Ellie in her bedroom that they're allowed in the living room again, which I instantly regret because by the time they barrel downstairs and immediately put on a music video channel, I am comfortably installed in a chair reading *Ghost World* for the thousandth time. They sprawl on the sofa, Ellie's fine brown hair fanning over the back. I curl up and let the sounds of the videos wash over me, my thigh muscles still burning from the skating. I let my eyes flow over the panels of *Ghost World*, my comfort read, and even though I know every scene, every character, the sound of the TV is distracting.

I give up on the book and open Instagram, expecting to scroll through holiday photos of various people from my year, but there's a message waiting for me in my inbox.

Hey, sorry if this is creepy but I saw you out running the other day in the park and just wanted to say you looked totally badass!

When I examine the little icon more closely, I see it's Liv, aka The Other Fat Girl. Huh! Now there's a surprise! I reread the message. I don't like the idea that people I know could be seeing me in my most disgusting moments, but . . . this is cool of her! I feel enthused and emboldened by her message, and decide now is the time to maybe hang out with another chubster.

I message her back and suggest we get together sometime, and she doesn't take long to reply with a yes. So we make a plan to meet next week at a café in Forest Hill. I don't have any fat friends! Maybe this is exactly what I need. Unless she turns out to be a huge bitch, in which case that is exactly not what I need. I'll reserve judgment.

I slip my phone back into my shorts pocket, and Mum reappears from the kitchen. "I've got some leftovers from that big order I did. Who wants a cupcake?"

"Me!" Sasha and I say in sync.

"Ellie?" Mum asks.

Ellie doesn't take her eyes off the screen. "No, thank you. My mum says cakes will make me fat."

Instantly the atmosphere shifts to one of pure tension. I don't want to look at Sasha. I barely want to look at Mum.

"Oh," she says. "Well, there are worse things to be."

Ellie just shrugs.

"No cake, then?" Mum checks.

Ellie shakes her head. As Mum is turning back to the kitchen to get one for me and Sasha, I hear Sasha say, "I don't want one either."

"But you just said you did?" Mum says, her voice strained, a little panicky.

"I was *joking*," she says, rolling her eyes and looking at Ellie for approval, who doesn't seem that interested.

"Are you sure?"

"I'm sure," she says.

As I eat my little pink-icing-topped cupcake, I have to try not to cry. I even feel a hot prickle of shame for eating it myself. It's just a cupcake! How is this happening to her already? How do they know so much? I say a silent thank-you to the cosmos for sending me a mum who didn't plant these thoughts in our little pliable brains, and I try to just . . . enjoy the cupcake. If they weren't meant to be enjoyed, then why are they so tasty? Riddle me that!

I keep stealing glances at Sasha, wondering what she's thinking. I can't kid myself anymore that it doesn't bother her at all. I guess I was in her position once, even though it feels like a long time ago. And I got to where I am now by, like, *aggressively* not letting it bother me. I had to really try to resist it, because it's easy to let it worm its way into your head and into your behavior and into your conversation. But I decided not to. I wanted to try to see if there was another way of doing things, if it was possible to have a different way of thinking about my body and about other people's bodies. I want that for Sasha so much.

"OK, you two, have fun," I say to Sasha and Ellie. "Mum, I'm going to Salma's!" I call to the kitchen.

"All right, will you be back for dinner?"

"Yes, I'll text you when I'm walking home," I say, shoving my keys into my pocket.

CHAPTER 15

When I get to Salma's twenty minutes later, April and Jessica are already there. April gives me a little salute in greeting. Jessica is lying on Salma's bed, dangling upside down so her braids are pooled on the floor like coiled blue snakes.

"Hey, girl," she says, righting herself.

Salma has gone straight from opening the door for me to clamping her phone into its holder on the tripod resting on her desk. "You ready for this?"

"Born ready," Jessica says, wiggling her shoulders in excitement.

Salma is filming a video for her Instagram reels where she's doing a full watercolor-painting-inspired eye makeup look on Jessica. She seats Jessica in the desk chair facing the window, beautiful sunlight streaming in.

"We're not in the background here, are we?" April asks, looking around furtively.

"Not if you stay up that end of the bed." She nods toward the headboard.

"We'll curl up here like little cats and stay out of the shot," I assure her.

"Are we allowed to talk?" April asks, clearly very perturbed by the whole prospect.

"Yes! It's a time-lapse video, so there won't be sound on it anyway."

"Phew!" I say.

Jessica laughs kindly. "Can you imagine Ruby trying to stay quiet for more than about five seconds?"

"Let's be fair—I think she could probably manage ten." April winks at me.

"Ugh! How rude!" I say indignantly, even though they're right.

Salma leans over her phone in the tripod, presses a button, and says, "Right, we're on," before getting to work on Jessica's face.

"Jessica," April says, "have you made any progress on your summer crush?"

"Joshua?" she asks.

"Yes, why, how many have you got?" I ask her.

"I only have eyes for him," she says, and I can see in the phone screen that she's smiling widely.

"Stop moving your face so much!" Salma tells her impatiently.

"All right!" Jessica complies, moving her mouth the bare minimum to tell us, "I'm meeting him in the park tomorrow."

"Ooooh! A date!" I say. "Hyped for you."

"And how's your thing with the ginger boy?" Jessica asks me, turning around to look at me and April sitting in pretzel-like positions on the bed. Salma taps her on the head with a makeup brush. "Oh my God, sorry!" Jessica says, knowing she is doing a bad job of being a model.

Salma looks at us over her shoulder, blowing a lock of shiny black hair out of her eyes. "Yeah, tell us more about this whole thing you've got going on. Boy, running, Dawson Dash, all of it. In detail."

I sigh, wondering how stupid it'll all sound when I say it out loud. "Well, I got into this whole thing with my brother—"

"Your fit brother," says Salma.

I will never understand what she sees in him. "Ugh, no, stop, it's just too disgusting!" I shudder. "I got into this whole thing with my brother about the bloody . . . Dawson Dash. He was doing some macho bullshit thing and basically said I couldn't run it because I'm fat, which *obviously* I was not going to tolerate. So I decided to enter, which means I have to train for it."

"I feel like I'm only just fully absorbing the fact that you're going to run the Dawson Dash this year. You, Ruby Morgan, who conjured up two periods a month to get out of PE?"

"The human body is a mysterious thing," I say, shrugging off my copious lies to the PE department of Dawson High. "And . . . yes, I am. I also said I could win it, which puts me in a *slightly* more dubious position . . ."

"Oh my days," says Salma, laughing and shaking her head as she works on Jessica's face. "I know when you say it, it sounds kind of crazy, but . . . I just believe you can, you know?"

I can't help but smile. "We don't have long between now and the race, so I'm just trying to get on with it, and it's going kind of OK so far." Well, I haven't died. Or thrown up again.

"So how does the ginger boy fit into the equation?" Jessica asks.

"Ollie. His name is Ollie. Anyway, he saw me out running when I went for the first time and said if I needed any, like, help, that I could ask him. And . . . unsurprisingly, I *do* need help."

"Plus a good excuse to hang out with a cute guy," says Jessica, raising her eyebrows suggestively, which earns her another tap with a makeup brush from Salma.

"As if! I look like absolute garbage when I run, so it's actually the worst-case scenario. Hanging out with a cute guy *specifically and exclusively* when you look like shit."

"Congratulations. You played yourself," Jessica says, grinning.

"I'm prioritizing winning my bet with my brother over my romantic interests. I think it's noble."

"So how often are you running?" Salma asks as she swirls a fluffy brush in some duck-egg-blue eye shadow before tapping it on the edge of her desk so it sends up a little puff of shimmer into the air like dust.

"Three times a week," I say. "Which sounds like a lot, but we're not actually *doing* that much yet."

"All in good time," April says philosophically.

"I think you're gonna smash it," says Jessica.

I sigh. "I hope so."

"How can you not if you're running three times a week?" Salma asks. "There's still, like, a month to go until the race."

I do not take this opportunity to tell her that I've still not actually run for more than three minutes at a time. I've got a long way to go! I know it!

"Do you think?"

"Yeah, I think," she says. "It's just practice. And time. And building up. You're so determined—there's no way you're not going to do this."

"I'm worried that it's, like, physically beyond me. Like, in my brain I *know* I can do it. But I just feel . . . this instinctive fear that I literally can't."

"All you can do is practice. That's actually all it is. Like me and makeup," she says, shrugging as she stands back and surveys her handiwork on Jessica's face.

"Yeah, I don't know if you're aware of this, but you're *really talented*," I say to Salma.

She just rolls her eyes. "Do you really think I was this good all along? No! You've known me for, like, five years!"

"I guess . . ." I say sheepishly.

"I wasn't doing this," she says, gesturing at Jessica's face, "a couple of years ago. I couldn't, because I just hadn't put the time in. It's not like I was born with a special skill." She shrugs. "You could do it. Any of you lot could do it. But you won't because it's not something you're *that* interested in."

"I guess not . . ."

"But running? If you're, like, mentally committed to it and you've got someone to keep you accountable and you're invested in the whole thing, then there's no reason why you can't do it."

"Yeah!" Jessica says triumphantly. "What she said!"

I flush with something like pride or happiness, even though I haven't really done anything yet. Just the fact that they think I can do it means a lot. I mean, I know I talked a big game to Jake about how I could definitely do it, no questions asked, but . . . it's still hard! Like, really hard!

But Salma's right. It's just a question of practice. Isn't it?

CHAPTER 16

"This is too easy," Jessica says, weaving backward to where Salma, April, and I are skating in circles around the tennis court in Mayow Park. "It's no fun!"

"You mean Joshua isn't here?" April says dryly.

"Not *just* that," Jessica says.

We slump against the green cage fence that separates the tennis courts from the path I've been pounding with Ollie.

Salma shields her eyes from the sun. "Hey, isn't that your mum and Sasha?" she says, looking to the path on the other side of the tennis courts. I get back up to my feet and skate over. Mum and Sasha are strolling through the sunny park, Mum in a floral sundress and sandals to match the glorious summer weather, but Sasha's in a hoodie and jeans.

"Mum!" I call to her. "Where are you off to?"

"Just to Lidl to get some bits," she calls back to me.

"Hey, Sash," I say to my sister. "Why are you wearing that when it's so hot?"

Mum exhales loudly. "Don't ask. I had the same conversation with her and couldn't persuade her out of it."

"I'm not hot. I'm fine." Sasha sulks, although she's visibly sweating. I don't like the look of this one bit.

"All right, well, I'll be coming home soon to change to . . . well, come back here and go running with Ollie."

"OK!" Mum shouts back, waving as I skate to where the other three are sipping from their water bottles.

"Gah!" I say as I join them on the ground. "I'm stressed about Sasha."

"Why?" Jessica asks.

"I'm worried she's, like . . . obsessed with the way she looks. It's feeling like she's just getting more and more self-conscious. Did you see what she was wearing? It's ridiculous. A hoodie?"

"Maybe she just wanted to wear a hoodie," Salma says, shrugging. I want to tell her, *No! I remember those days, I remember those feelings, before I figured out how I really felt about my body, before I figured out that I didn't have to believe it was bad and wrong! I remember never wanting to show my fat arms or my thighs, covering up in the summer, always hiding under a towel at the beach! I've been there!*

"I'm not so sure . . ." is what I say instead.

"Could you talk to her about it?" April asks, adjusting her wrist protectors.

"Not really . . . I don't know . . . I don't want to make it worse."

It's very obvious that I'm not going to get any good advice out of this lot, even though they're my best friends. This is just something I'll have to tackle on my own.

We skate around the tennis courts until an intense-looking man with gray hair announces that *actually* he's booked the court for five o'clock, so can we please leave? And then I realize I only have half an hour to get home and changed and sort myself out in time for my run with Ollie.

But in true Ruby Morgan efficiency, I make it, and I'm back

outside at five thirty, in time to psych myself up for today's run. And, boy, do I need to psych myself up.

Five minutes. It's only five minutes. I can do this. It's five minutes. What's five minutes? It's nothing. It would pass in the blink of an eye if I wasn't running. But I am running! Or rather, I will be. Every time I think about how *extremely long* five minutes is, I'm then hit with the reality of just how big this task is, and how it's looming in, what, four weeks now? Because if I'm going to run the Dawson Dash, then it's going to take me more than five minutes. But I'll get there. I have to get there.

"You really think I can do this?" I ask Ollie as we walk down the slope into Mayow Park.

"I don't think so," he says, pausing meaningfully. "I *know* so." And he says it with such conviction that I genuinely believe that he believes in me, which is very hot of him. I do wish he would be a little bit less hot. A little bit less full lips and cute dimples and gentle brown eyes and deep auburn hair. Less of that, please.

"But it's so hot today," I say, already on the verge of breaking a sweat.

"There's not a lot I can do about that, Roo," he says, and hearing him use my nickname makes me feel all soft and squishy inside and I have to try really hard not to smile.

"I guess not."

"OK, let's just get to it," he says, setting the timer on his phone. "Don't think too much about it. Don't think about how long you have to run for, just focus on how you're feeling in the moment. And I bet you'll find it's more manageable than you're expecting."

Somehow I doubt that.

"Let's go!" he says in his infectiously enthusiastic way, and before I know it, we're running. Slowly. But running.

O n e f o o t i n f r o n t o f t h e o t h e r o n e f o o t i n f r o n t o f t h e o t h e r o n e f o o t i n f r o n t o f t h e o t h e r o n e f o o t i n f r o n t o f t h e o t h e r

Plod, plod, plod, I go on the track around the park. Ollie keeps checking over his shoulder to make sure I'm still alive, periodically slowing down a little to match my pace. I do wish he wouldn't keep looking at me in my moments of particular red-faced breathlessness.

After what easily feels like five minutes, I pant, "Are we nearly done yet?"

"I'm not telling you anything," he says, not panting at all. Classic fit-person behavior. "You don't need to know. Just keep going!"

I huff indignantly but do what he says and keep jogging. I feel like my lungs are going to give up on me any minute now, like they're just going to get overworked and decide *nope, no more!* How hasn't it been five minutes already? And I have to do this again *two* more times today!

"Stop!" he says, grinning broadly. "You did it!"

"I . . . did . . . it . . ." I say, grinding to a halt, trying to get my breath back and failing.

"Don't stop—keep walking! Gotta get some of that sweet active recovery going," he says, his eyes wide and encouraging, like a puppy that's begging to be fed.

"Ugh! Whatever happened to *passive* recovery?"

"It went out of fashion," he says before taking a sip of water from his bottle, which reminds me I should probably do the same. When I go to take a gulp of water, I find that it hits my mouth at the exact same moment my body has decided I need to breathe in, causing me to choke and splutter in the *most* mortifying way.

Ollie slaps me on the back. "Are you all right?"

"I'm fine," I say once my airways are clear enough to speak.

"Not trying to get out of doing the next two runs today?"

"Would I?" I say. "Would I do that?"

"Never," he says, smiling. I wish he wouldn't do that so much.

We walk in silence for what feels like a few seconds, then he announces it's time to set off again. That was two minutes?

I don't feel ready! I feel less ready than I did before the first one because now I know that five minutes really does feel like *ages*. I start the next run with what can only be described as a very bad attitude. But, against all odds, it's . . . ever so slightly bearable? Not good but bearable. I can . . . do it. I can. I'm doing it. I am doing it! Is the five minutes up yet? No? Oh. Suppose I'd better keep going.

"Stop!" Ollie says after an amount of time that feels like it could have been either thirty seconds or ten minutes. "Slow down and we'll have a walk before the next one."

"That was . . . better!" I say, positively surprised.

"Right?! That's a little thing called progress."

"I've heard of that."

"You should *expect* to be getting better every time you run at this stage! I don't know why you're so surprised that, you know, what we're doing is actually working!"

I feel a bit stupid. He's right! I'm doing this so that one day (specifically the fifth of September) I can run five kilometers. So it makes sense that I have to be taking steps toward that. I guess I just never thought that I, Ruby Morgan, could actually . . . do this?

"Still got one run left today," he says.

"I haven't forgotten," I reassure him.

"Have some water and try to get your breathing back," he says, which makes me go red because I don't want him to notice that I'm so out of breath. I'm not sure how I would get away with that, but I liked maintaining the fiction in my own little brain. "But be careful! That water can be dangerous!"

I do what he says and take a sip, very delicately, forcing my body not to breathe in at the same time. "See?" I say when I don't choke.

"It's like I said! Progress! You ready to go again?" he asks when we've walked to the café.

"Born ready," I say with a confidence that's half real, half fake.

As I set off on my slow stomp of our last five-minute run, I think about Liv spotting me and how self-conscious I feel about people seeing me run. I hate it—and I hate that I hate it! I should be better than that! I shouldn't care! But I do! I do care! But then again, Liv said I looked badass, which is nice. I hope she's telling the truth and doesn't actually think I must be having some sort of meltdown. I wonder what it's going to be like to hang out with her tomorrow. I hope it's not awkward.

"Stop!" says Ollie, which comes as a surprise to me.

"Oh!" I say. "I'd sort of zoned out." It's not that I'm not out of breath or sweating or that my leg muscles aren't aching. It's more that those things didn't consume my every thought for every second of that run. I was able to get distracted.

"See? It's like I said: progress."

"I guess if I just get a bit better every time . . ." I say, thinking aloud, while also trying to regulate my ragged breathing.

"Yeees?"

"Then one day . . . I'll end up being . . . a lot better?"

"You've got it!" he says. "I told you that you could do this."

"Maybe I can, you know?"

He looks at me with such intense kindness in his big brown eyes that I nearly melt into a sweaty puddle on the path. "You can." And he puts his hand on the back of my neck for a few seconds, even though it's definitely sweaty. It's probably just a bro-ish gesture of running solidarity, but it feels . . . intimate. I'm not used to him touching me.

Ugh! I wish the time we spent together wasn't specifically the time when I look the absolute worst. Is this what a catch-22 is? He only ever sees me when I'm looking like garbage, but the only reason we hang out at all is in pursuit of the thing that makes me look like garbage. Surely that's what whoever wrote *Catch-22* was thinking of when he wrote it: cute fat girls wanting to get to know their hot neighbor.

"Mum was so happy with your delivery skills, by the way," I say through breath that's slowly, slowly returning to normal.

"Oh yeah?"

"Yeah! She said you didn't even take much longer than Dad used to, and he was driving a car," I say. "But then again he was probably using the time out of the house to have long romantic chats with what's-her-name." As soon as I say it, I wish I hadn't.

"Oh?" Ollie says gently.

I swallow. I think about it. He opened up to me, didn't he? Maybe it wouldn't kill me to be honest with him too.

"Yeah, it was a whole thing," I say. I still don't really know how to talk about it. I've barely talked about it with April, but I've always given her the basics, and there's no real need to talk about it with my mum and Jake and Sasha because Mum and Jake know what's up and Sasha doesn't need to know the ins and outs of it. But I try to find the right words. "Some woman he met online . . . and then it was, like . . . why were you even looking to meet women online? Like, it doesn't happen by accident, does it? You sort of have to go looking?"

Ollie nods thoughtfully, like he doesn't want to interrupt me.

"Anyway, she lives in Manchester. Which means *he* lives in Manchester now."

"Shit," he says.

"Yeah . . . It wasn't really something anyone saw coming. I mean, I didn't. Like, I knew they were arguing, but all parents argue, don't they? That wasn't anything too shocking. But then they were arguing more and more, but even that didn't seem like enough to break them up. And then . . . this. Which definitely *was* enough to break them up."

"I'm really sorry," he says, and it sounds like he means it.

I shrug. "It's OK." And then I wonder why I'm pretending. "It's actually really hard. I don't feel like I know how to be with him anymore. And I know my mum is really . . . yeah, just . . . finding it hard." I don't feel right talking about her, so I just leave it at that.

"It's still new," Ollie says. "Of course it's hard."

"I guess . . ." I say. And I realize I don't want to talk about it anymore after that. Saying out loud that it's hard and that I hate it was enough.

We walk in silence the rest of the way home. But when we get to our houses, Ollie stops by the gate to mine. "I just wanted to say, I'm really enjoying this, you know?"

I smile, glad I'm not completely wasting his time on my

potentially ridiculous athletic escapade. "Yeah, me too. I really appreciate it. I don't know what I would be doing if I was going running on my own."

"I mean, just in general . . ." He thinks for a second. "Anyway, I'll see you on Wednesday, yeah?"

I nod resolutely. "Yeah, I'll see you then."

Just in general, you say?

CHAPTER 17

When I get ready to meet Liv the next day, I feel like I'm preparing for a date. I keep pulling clothes out of my wardrobe and putting them on and looking at myself in the mirror and trying to see myself through Liv's eyes. Which is hard because, well, I don't really know her, do I? Finally I pull out an oversize T-shirt that I could tuck into high-waisted jeans and add my shell-toe sneakers. Neutral. Neither here nor there, you know? A winning formula.

As I stomp down the stairs, I check my phone to see if Liv has canceled on me at the last minute, but instead there's a text from April.

Want to come over later?

When? I'm meeting someone soon but could do this evening.

Idk like 6. What is this "someone"?

I'll tell you about it later omg

So you are coming over?

Ye

K

I call out to Mum that I won't be back for dinner and head out. I'm running a little late now, so I pick up the pace along the main road and around the corner to where I'm meeting Liv. When I arrive, she's not already there, so I loiter outside and take out my phone to waste time.

I'm really missing you, Roo. I know we haven't been able to catch up for a while, but can we have Wednesday-night pizza on Zoom next week like we used to?

It's Dad. A lump forms in my throat at the sight of it. I want to reply, saying, *We didn't used to eat the pizza on Zoom. We used to eat it together in the living room.* But I know I shouldn't. I can't keep putting him off. So I agree to it.

"Hey!" Liv says, breaking me out of my thoughts. When I look up, I see she's wearing . . . an oversize T-shirt tucked into jeans with shell-toe trainers.

"Oh my God, did we . . . ? Are we twins?" I say, laughing possibly more than is necessary, but the nerves of meeting up with a new person and the stress of Sasha and my dad has put me *right* on edge.

She laughs too. "At least my T-shirt is white and yours is black?" she offers, smiling to reveal slightly overlapping front teeth. Despite our mostly matching outfits, the only other thing Liv and I have in common physically is the fact that we're both fat. Her hair is pale blond and curly, forming a bouncy halo around her head. She wears glasses, thick-rimmed and square, the contrast between the sugary-soft hair and the glasses giving her an almost cartoonishly graphic look. And she's really tall. Like, I'm not short, but I'm not tall either. But Liv is *tall*.

"Shall we . . . ?" she asks, gallantly holding the door open for me. It's like she's decided this won't be awkward. She just won't let it. Maybe that's the kind of person she is. Sending people messages saying they look cool is quite a bold move, so why *would* she be awkward?

We go inside and order iced coffees. Liv asks if they have sugar syrup and they say no, just regular sugar, which Liv clearly thinks is ridiculous but accepts it anyway. We sit down at a big wooden table under a Moroccan metal hanging lamp. I stab my red-and-white-striped paper straw into the top of the cup. Liv does the same. And it's only now that we're sitting down, face-to-face, that the awkwardness sets in. Neither of us looks up from our drinks for a few seconds, unsure who's meant to speak now that we're inside in this strange new one-on-one situation.

I take a deep breath and decide to say something, but I haven't decided what when I open my mouth. "So . . ." I say, but Liv says something at the same time. "No, you go!" I say, knowing whatever I was about to offer was of zero conversational value.

"No, I was just going to say . . ." she says, taking a sip of the iced coffee. I never knew she had such a scratchy voice. Have I really never spoken to her properly before today? "I guess this was a kind of weird thing for me to do."

"No!" I say, realizing how keen I am for this to work, for us to become actual friends. "It's not weird at all. It's really cool. I think, anyway."

"I just saw you out in Wells Park and thought . . . Well, she looks cool, you know? And, like, either you're running for a weight-loss thing or you're just doing it, and if it's a weight-loss thing, maybe *you* could do with having a fat friend, or if it's not, then maybe *I* could do with having a fat friend."

I'm completely caught off-guard by how straightforward she is. I'm not used to hearing the word *fat* said out loud to me in a way that isn't meant to hurt me or make me feel bad about myself. But I wish I *was*. I can't help smiling. "It's not a weight-loss thing. I'm training for the Dawson Dash with my neighbor, the guy I was with." I try not to let my crush on Ollie show on my face. And then I wonder why that's so important to me. April tried to make me understand I'm allowed to like people, but I haven't quite gotten there yet.

"So, yeah, he's helping me kind of . . . get ready for the race. I tried to do it on my own, but I didn't really know what I was doing."

"This shit is intimidating! All of it!"

"All of what?" I ask.

"Exercise! Sports! I'm extremely relaxed about the way my body looks, but trying to get involved in stuff like this takes a lot of . . . willpower."

"It's like they don't want us there," I say, realizing maybe I'm right.

She swirls the coffee around in the cup. "Ugh, how is sugar even meant to dissolve in iced coffee? This is a joke. Anyway, the other girls on the field hockey team always looked at me like, *What's she doing here?* at first, but I showed them who's boss."

"Oh . . . that's cool." I definitely want to know more about what Liv showing someone who's boss looks like.

But before I can ask, she says, "Like I said, you looked badass. So determined."

"The idea of people seeing me out and about doing my little runs is incredibly cringe, but if you think I looked cool, then maybe I did."

"You did," Liv says, taking off her glasses to clean them on her T-shirt.

"You want to join us?" I ask, infused with the good vibes of hanging out with Liv. But I instantly worry I should have asked Ollie first and wonder if I would rather she says yes or no.

"Maybe!" she says brightly in a way that tells me she won't, as she slides her glasses back onto her nose. "I'll think about it."

"I guess you probably don't, like, *need* to . . ."

"It's not like that. It's just I'm more of a solitary runner. Lone wolf. If I *have* to run, you know?"

"Huh," I say, nodding. "But you run in field hockey, right?"

"Yeah, but never that far. Short distances? Little breaks in between. Running for more than a few minutes is hard! That's why I respect you so much for doing it, and for doing it with someone else! When the girls on the team do their fitness shit outside of, like, actual field hockey, I always avoid joining them." I want to know more about this, but before I can ask, she turns the conversation back to me. "So. Why *are* you doing it?"

I swallow, feeling ridiculous already. "It's kind of . . . stupid, I guess? But, uh, my brother won it a couple of years ago, and then it turns out my dad won it too, years ago, and my brother is a real dick and is always on me about losing weight, and recently I've started seeing how body . . . *stuff* is affecting our little sister who's not even at secondary school yet, so I figured . . ." It does sound stupid! Just listen to me! "I figured if I entered, I could show *both* of them that I don't need to lose weight to do whatever I want."

"Doesn't sound stupid to me," Liv says. "Those are two pretty good motivators."

"Spite and love," I say, smiling.

"Exactly. So what's going on with your sister?"

"Well, she's ten. She's called Sasha. She's starting at Dawson next year. And she's . . . well, she's chubby too. And she's so cute and kind and good, but it's already feeling like none of that matters because she's not thin. Like, matters to *her*, I mean. My parents have never been on at her about it, and I definitely haven't, but it's coming from somewhere. My brother doesn't help, but at least he's not around loads these days, except for precisely *right now* because it's the summer holidays. I just . . . don't really know how to help her. I don't know how to talk to her about it without making her feel more self-conscious, you know?"

"I know exactly what you mean. Like, a few years ago, if someone had tried to talk to me about my weight, even in a properly positive way, I would have been mortified," she says, covering her face with her hands.

"Yeah, like, *Oh my God, they've noticed I'm fat!*" I say, laughing at how ridiculous that idea is.

"Like, of *course* they've noticed! It's the way I look! It's not like I can hide it, right? But I would still have been mortified."

"Exactly!" I say. "So I don't really know how to deal with it with her."

"Hmmm," Liv says.

"And I . . ." I'm looking intently at my stripy straw, then I look up and say the thing I've been thinking but haven't been able to say yet. "Well, I don't really feel like I can talk to my friends about it because . . ."

"They might not get it," Liv says.

"Yeah."

She pushes her chair out a little and crosses her legs. "I feel like shit changed for me when I stopped seeing fat as this unique characteristic that was, I don't know, the be-all and end-all."

"How do you mean?" I ask, feeling like I should understand what she's saying but knowing that I don't.

"I just changed how I thought about it. I was just, like . . . well, it's human variation. It's literally just human variation. The way we talk about it, you would think it was the *worst* thing in the whole world, something that affected your personality and your behavior and whatever. But it's not. It's just a variation in our appearance. So you don't have to talk about it with your sister like it's this big scary thing with all the stigma attached, you know? You can just present it to her as this neutral thing like hair color or whatever. Which it is."

I smile. I can't help it. I smile because it makes so much sense to me. It feels true to me, because it *is* true.

"I stopped hating myself—no, wait, that's not true. I never hated myself," I say, thinking out loud. "I stopped *worrying* about my body when I started following all these amazing people on Instagram and TikTok and whatever, but part of me was still kind of like . . . am I wrong? Is it actually bad? But it's not, is it? It's just a pretty basic difference. Or . . . what was it you called it? Variation."

"I don't think it's bad at all. Shit . . ." Liv says, shaking her head and laughing a little. "I honestly don't know where I would be without the Internet. I'd probably still be hoping that one day, *one day* I'll have the body for a bikini! Or that one day I'll be able to try out for the field hockey team!"

"I hadn't even *thought* about that," I say, trying not to shudder with horror. "Can you imagine?"

"No, like, I literally can't. You're the only other fat girl in our year at school, and it's taken me, what, five years to even talk to you properly, so where else are we meant to get this good stuff infused into our brains if not on the Internet?"

"It's funny, you know what you said about people thinking being fat was something that affected your personality and behavior, but now you don't think it is," I say thoughtfully. "I think it kind of does affect those things, but, I don't know, not in a bad way? Like it sort of . . . makes you wonder what other stuff is just sold to us as fact. Stuff we think is normal." I shrug, embarrassed. "I don't know."

"No, you're right," Liv says. "Just having someone around who can try to counteract all that bullshit is really powerful. You're doing a good job with your sister. I just know it."

I feel a little lightness in my chest when I hear that. I can't help laughing with the relief of having someone to talk to. "Thanks. Sorry, I get kind of wound up about all this stuff and it's just nice to be able to let it out."

She smiles warmly. "See? I knew this would be fun."

And we talk, and talk, and talk. About graphic novels, and our families, and school, and cool fat girls to follow on the Internet, and what we want to do after sixth form. The café empties around us, until a nervous-looking man comes over and says, "Actually, we're closing now . . . so if you wouldn't mind?"

I gasp and check the time on my phone. "Shit!" I say. "I'm meant to be at April's by now! Lemme just text her." I drop her a text, saying I'll be there soon.

"April, eh?" Liv says as she gets up from the table, and when I look up from my phone, I'm sure I catch the end of a smile.

"Yeah, April Nowinski. I don't know if you know her. I guess not."

"I don't, but . . ." She smiles properly now, blushing a little. "You know how even though we didn't really *know* each other we were, like, *aware* of each other? Same for queer people."

"Oh yeah, I guess," I say.

“She was with Juliet last year, yeah? Who’s now with Rosie, right? Or is that, like, confidential information that I’ve just blurted out?”

It’s my turn to hold the door open for her, but I feel kind of sad that we’re leaving, that it’s over rather than just beginning. It feels like we’ve been there no time at all, but it’s actually been *hours*. “Nah, it’s definitely public intel. April’s not happy about it, but it’s not like she doesn’t know.”

“So April’s not . . . uh . . .” Suddenly Liv looks awkward, which is a departure from the assurance she’s had since our conversation got flowing. “She’s not moved on to someone else already?”

I shake my head and try not to smile. I don’t want her to feel even *more* awkward.

“Huh,” she says, like it’s just a piece of faintly interesting information.

“Well,” I say, gesturing toward the other side of Forest Hill Station, “she lives that way, so I’m heading under the bridge.”

“I live back that way,” she says, nodding in the direction of the Horniman Museum. “So . . .”

“So I guess I’ll see you again soon?”

“Definitely.”

We hug, and it feels nice to have someone put their arms around me, knowing they’re not thinking, *Wow, there’s just so much of her!* And we go our separate ways.

“Hey!” Liv calls to me a few seconds later. I turn and look at her over my shoulder. “Don’t forget to tell April what a fun time you had with me!”

“I won’t!” I say.

CHAPTER 18

April's room is already shrouded in darkness when I finally make it there half an hour later.

"Oh my God, where have you been?" she asks impatiently from her comfy-looking position on her bed. "I was hiding in the wardrobe waiting for you to arrive so I could jump out on you, but I got bored and gave up."

"You haven't done that in so long that you'd probably have killed me."

"So," she says, moving over to make room for me next to her. "Tell me all."

"All what?" I say, feigning ignorance.

"What have you been doing? What is this intrigue? Did you have a date with Ollie? A proper one?"

"Jesus! No! I wish, God. I was with Liv."

"Liv Bennett?" She sounds curious, and it hits me how much I don't want April to say she thinks Liv sucks or she heard some rumor about her or whatever. In the space of an afternoon, she's become someone I want to be friends with. The way I'm friends with April and Salma and Jessica.

"Yeah," I say.

"Whoa! What's she like?"

"So fucking cool," I say. "Like, properly amazing."

"She's too cool. Like, way too cool. I want to know everything."

"Why? You like her?"

She looks shifty. "Maybe."

"Is it?"

"Don't you think she's so hot? Like just the way she's so tall and has that hair."

"April! I have never heard you talk like this about someone! You're always playing it cool!"

She shrugs. "So what? Let me live my truth!"

"She . . ." I smile, enjoying the power of knowing a little something. "She seemed interested in you."

"What?!" April gasps, delighted. "Are you joking?"

"I am not joking! That would be so mean!"

"Wow . . . OK . . . wow . . ." she says, trying to come to terms with this juicy new information. "Wow."

"I said I didn't think she was your type," I say, trying to keep a straight face and looking at her out of the corner of my eye.

"What?! Why would you do that?" she says, hitting me on the arm.

"Oh my God, I'm joking! I didn't say anything! I didn't know you were even aware of her existence!"

"How can you not be? She's about six feet tall and extremely hot and also a confirmed gay. How come you haven't spoken to her before now?"

I sigh. "I think it's because we were both a bit self-conscious about gravitating toward the only other fat girl in our year. I don't know, maybe I'm projecting. Maybe Liv never thought about me at all. But yeah . . . I think I would have felt . . . a bit embarrassed about it? Like, back in Year Seven, you know. And then the longer it went on, the weirder it would have been to be, like, *Oh no, wait, actually I do want to be friends with you because I'm not embarrassed about being a fat bitch these days*, you know?"

"Yeah, I see what you're saying," April says, nodding thoughtfully. "Like, for ages I didn't want to *do* anything that would, like, implant the idea that I'm gay in people's minds. So I definitely didn't want anything to do with Rosie Wood when she was the first one to come out after everyone was always on at her about being a lesbian, which, like, she *was*, but that's not the point. I didn't want to get targeted by association."

"Now you just don't want anything to do with Rosie because she stole your girl," I say, hoping, maybe, that I'm allowed to say that now that April's distracted by the idea of Liv.

"Exactly."

What April and I do when it's just us, when Jessica and Salma aren't there, is watch horror films. They don't have to be new. They don't have to be good. They just have to be horror films.

"Do you want something you've seen before or something new?" she asks, opening her laptop.

"Let's watch *The Ring*," I say, smiling and remembering how little April had slept after we watched it the first time.

"The American one, yeah?" she says hopefully.

"No! Japanese!"

She covers her face with her hands. "Fine," she says, looking for it on her various Internet haunts. We settle under the duvet of her single bed, squished together, clinging on to each other for dear life when we get scared, which is often, because even though we love watching horror films, more than anything, we love being scared together. April writhes with sheer terror when they make you watch the actual videotape that's killing the kids in the film, digging her mercifully short nails into my arm.

"Aren't you scared to walk home alone?" she says, unusually wide-eyed, when I announce that I'm going to leave, after we've had an excellent bowl of her dad's carbonara.

"Because I think a creepy long-haired girl is going to walk weirdly at me out of the darkness? No, because it's still light outside."

"You're so brave," she says flatly, returning to her usual April self. She hugs me. "Are you going to see Liv again soon?"

"I don't have any plans to, but I'm sure I will," I say. "Want me to put in a good word? If I see her again, that is."

"Oh my God, no! But maybe you can introduce us sometime."

"Maybe I can," I say, raising my eyebrows suggestively. "See you, dude."

As I walk home, I feel a little buoyant, like I'm looking forward to running again. I'm thinking that maybe, just maybe, I'll succeed.

CHAPTER 19

I brush a bit of mascara on my lashes and try to tame my hair before I *extremely* casually slink downstairs.

"Oh, hi, Ollie," I say. "I didn't know you were here!" Which is, quite obviously, a lie.

It's Tuesday, time for his local delivery route.

"Hey, you," he says, looking up from the boxes he's piling into the trailer and smiling at me.

I try not to smile back too hard, but it's difficult! He makes me want to smile! You know, when he's not making me want to die when we're out running.

"What are you up to, Roo?" Mum asks, but before I can answer, the door slams and Jake thuds in.

"God, it's scorching out there. The pub's going to be rammed again tonight," he says, taking a swig from his water bottle. The absurd little vest he's using to wipe away the sweat on his brow tells me he's been for a run. "Oh, sorry to interrupt. What are you lot up to?" He looks at Ollie with suspicion.

"Jake," says Mum, "this is Ollie. He's helping me with the deliveries since you didn't seem that interested in getting involved. He lives next door. Ollie, this is Jake, Ruby's brother."

They nod at each other, and then Ollie gets back to work. Jake is taking off his trainers in the hall, and I'm sitting awkwardly in the armchair, wondering if I should be helping or if that would just be annoying. I pick up the copy of *Persepolis* by Marjane Satrapi that I'd left on the side table next to the armchair last time I was loitering down here, reading. I flip through the pages, trying to find where I was before, while also keeping an ear on the conversation in case they talk about anything interesting.

"So how are things going with Ruby's challenge?" Mum asks Ollie brightly. I guess this counts as something interesting, but I don't look up from my book just yet.

"You know what, she's actually doing amazingly." He looks over at me in the chair with an expression of genuine pride.

I sigh loudly. "You don't need to lie to her, Ollie." My eyes are back down on the page.

"I'm not lying!" he says, laughing. "I really think you're doing amazingly. You haven't given up! That's half the battle! You'll be ready for the race in no time."

"That's because there *is* no time!" I say, dropping the book into my lap and covering my face with my hands.

"We'll need to get a bit more intense. A bit more serious. But there's time. It's all in your head."

Jake snorts from the bottom of the stairs, his hand on the banister. "It's not really, though."

The atmosphere tightens.

"Well, I mean . . ." Ollie says, and clears his throat. "I would kind of disagree. I think a lot of this stuff is psychological."

"That's bollocks," says Jake, shaking his head.

"Jake!" Mum says. "Go upstairs and have a shower before your shift and leave us alone—we're working."

"Whatever . . ." he says, taking the stairs two at a time.

"So," Mum says, clapping her hands together like she's trying to dispel the bad vibes, "you've got the addresses, but do you need me to print them for you?"

Ollie smiles. "No, it's OK. I've made a map of the route already."

"Aren't you clever?" she says, glancing at me, like he's anything to do with me personally.

"Just trying to be smart with this—keep my time down," Ollie says, clipping on his bike helmet.

"You're such a help, honestly," Mum says.

"See you tomorrow, Ruby? Same time? Five thirty?"

I'm about to tell him that's fine, when Mum interjects. "Aren't you doing your thing with Dad tomorrow?"

"What thing?" I say before remembering. "Oh, yeah, Zoom pizza. That's at seven . . . so maybe we could do five? Is that OK?"

Ollie shrugs. "Fine with me. As long as you come with your game face on," he says, smiling that extremely delicious wide smile of his.

"Game face will be fully engaged, I promise."

"I just want to see you smash it! We're stepping up tomorrow."

"I don't know if I like the sound of that," I say, but I smile despite myself. "I made this new friend the other day—Liv—and she's really made me feel, you know, *motivated*. To make this all work."

"That's great! I'm glad I'm not the only one who thinks you're going to smash it. All right, I'll see you then," he says, giving me a little salute. "Or maybe I'll see you later when I come back to drop off the trailer thing. If you're lucky."

I can't help but blush. Mum shoots me a look, and I implore her with my most intense eye contact of all time not to say *a word*.

"See you later, Ollie!" she trills merrily. The door closes behind him.

"Well!" she says.

"Well what?"

"Just . . . well!" She's grinning like the Cheshire Cat.

"I don't know what you're talking about."

"He was flirting! He wants to see you later!" she says over her shoulder as she heads for the kitchen.

"I don't think so, matey," I say to her, lifting myself out of the chair and getting to my feet. No, I *don't* think so, and I can't *let* myself think so, but that doesn't stop the butterflies fluttering around my chest at the thought of it. Or the warm glow that someone would think he could like me, even if that someone is my mum.

"Here," she says, throwing me a dark-chocolate-and-banana cookie from the counter. "I made extra."

I take a bite. "Nice one! Maybe even . . . your finest work yet?"

Nibbling on my cookie and thinking about Ollie, as I so often do these days, I knock on Jake's door but don't wait for him to tell me to come in. "What was that about?" I ask.

He's sitting on his bed, rubbing his head with a towel post-shower. "What?"

"You know, telling Ollie he was talking bollocks. Someone you literally only just met?"

"Well, he was," he says, shrugging. "If you're in shape, you can do this stuff. If you're not, you can't. It's not in your head. That's just stupid."

"So you think I'm doomed to fail this?"

He smirks at me. "Yeah, I do actually. But I'm looking forward to seeing you try."

"How can you be so sure I'm going to fail?" I ask, trying not to flare my nostrils in irritation. I don't want him to know how much he gets to me.

"Because look at you," he says, throwing his towel on the floor. "You're clearly not taking it seriously at all."

"What?"

"If you gave a shit about it, you wouldn't be eating cookies every day," he says, rolling his eyes.

"I give a shit about it *and* I'm eating cookies every day. I'd rather die than drink that protein-powder nonsense, if that's what you mean."

"Well, yeah, that's pretty clear, isn't it? Anyway, when you change your mind about all this feminist body nonsense, I'll make you a protein shake." His expression and his tone are pure condescension.

"I'm not *going* to change my mind."

He shrugs. "Whatever. But you can't run five kilometers looking like *that*. It's just a fact."

I don't argue with him anymore. There's no point. The more I talk to him, the more I have to listen to the stuff he says, which is stuff I *know* people think about my body, or bodies like mine, but I don't need to *hear* it all the time. I know it was a stupid challenge to take on, but I really thought I could do it. Sure, I have my ups and downs and my confidence wobbles, but . . . I thought I could. You know, with a bit of practice and dedication.

When Ollie rings the doorbell later to drop off the trailer, I don't go downstairs to see him. I'm not in the mood. I just stay in my room. I can see him from out of my window. He doesn't hop over the low dividing wall between our front gardens to go straight back to his house; instead he walks to the end of the little path, through the creaking rusty gate, and looks back over his shoulder, like he's wondering if I'll appear in the doorway at any moment. No. It's more than that. Like he's *hoping* I will.

CHAPTER 20

Ugh. Wednesday. I've been dreading today. Not one, but two reasons to dread it. Two! Whatever happened to days with zero reasons for dread?

My reasons are this: Firstly, I have to run for TWENTY MINUTES nonstop. Did you ever hear of such a thing? Me? Ruby Morgan running for a whole twenty minutes? This is a bit of an escalation, is it not? Well, that's what I said to Ollie on Monday. He had me running for eight minutes nonstop, which was, let's be honest, not great, followed by a five-minute walk, which was much nicer, and then we did eight minutes of running again. He tried to talk to me in the second run to check that I was doing all right, but I physically could not chat. No way. And then at the end, he announced that today we're "stepping things up" and doing twenty minutes without a break in the middle! An outrage, if you ask me.

And then . . . the second reason. It's the day of Zoom pizza with Dad. Sasha and Jake are now involved, which might make it less awkward, but I'm really not looking forward to it one bit.

"Is your brother always like that?" Ollie asks, trying to sound good-natured and lighthearted but clearly thrown by Jake being so dismissive of him yesterday.

"Kind of, yeah . . . It's sort of his thing. He thinks because he works out all the time, he's king of the world and all the rest of us mere mortals are just slobs and fools."

Ollie laughs gently. "Well . . . I'm glad you don't let him get to you, I guess."

As he says this, I'm struck by the realization that if I really didn't let him get to me, I wouldn't be in this situation. I'm only doing this training because he *does* get to me. I wish he *didn't* have the power to get under my skin like this, but he does. "If you haven't already noticed, I *am* rather a fan of doing my own thing," I say, not feeling like getting into the intricacies of my family dynamics and relationship with my body with Ollie right now.

"OK," he says, clapping his hands together in a businesslike fashion. "Instead of running around parks like we have been, because we're going for longer today, we're going to go along some roads as well."

"Hilly roads?" I ask anxiously.

"I'll try to keep the hilly roads to a minimum," he says, smiling. "I've got a plan, so just follow me. I know where we're going." We walk to the top of the hill before the road slopes down again toward Mayow Park. "Ready?" he asks.

"Ready to run for twenty minutes nonstop, you mean?"

"Yeah . . . but don't think of it like that. Just take every step as it comes."

I swallow. I really don't feel ready at all. My head feels full of dark gray clouds. But maybe I'll surprise myself. "Let's go," I say a little wearily.

Ollie looks at me with a slightly worried expression but sets the timer on his phone anyway, and we get going.

We run along that road, past school, empty for the summer

holidays. So far, so good; I'm still running. When we reach the end of the road, we turn down the road on the other side of the park and run a lap around the outer path. Still going. How many minutes has it been? Not even close to half, I bet. As we pass the playground, something in me starts to slip away. A bit of tenacity. A bit of motivation. If it was ever there in the first place. But I press on, following Ollie through the park. We head back out of the gate where we came in, and then back past the road we first ran down before turning off on the road that leads to the little alley where April lives. But I'm struggling. I just don't see how I'm going to be able to finish this. There are so many minutes between me and the end. So many meters left to force my legs to run. So many breaths to take while I'm pushing my body to do something I don't want to do right now.

Screw this. I can't do it. It's not happening.

I grind to a halt. Relief floods through my calves. But not my brain. As soon as I slow down, I bitterly wish I hadn't. I could have kept going, couldn't I? Maybe?

"You OK?" Ollie asks me over his shoulder before stopping himself and turning back toward me.

"I just . . . couldn't . . ." I pant, my chest heaving.

"All right, it's all right," he says, nodding.

"Shit . . ." I say, doubled over. "Maybe I can't do this."

"Look, Ruby, please, please don't panic. It was a big jump. Maybe too big a jump." He looks at his phone. "We were at fifteen minutes, and that's a huge achievement in itself."

"Ugh, it's all just such a waste of time. I'm just wasting your time, aren't I?"

"Not at all," he says. "You've come so far already, and obviously you can do what you want—you can give up anytime—but

I think it would be a mistake to pack it in now, after one bump in the road." He's looking at me with so much kindness, I don't think I *could* give up now.

I stand up from my doubled-over position and look around. "I think this is where Liv's house is." I frown, trying desperately to get my breath back. "Quick, let's get out of here—I don't want to run into anyone *else* I know looking like this."

"Ah, you look fine," Ollie says, nudging me reassuringly.

I sigh. "I guess there's always Friday to try it one more time." The thought of running again makes me feel sick at this point, but maybe I'll be in the mood for it again by then.

"Actually, no," he says, looking guilty. "I'm away this weekend, so we won't be able to go out again until Monday."

Amid the general bad vibes of today, and the specific bad vibes of completely failing at this run, the disappointment hits me, and then the embarrassment at feeling disappointed. It's only a few days! Chill out, Ruby!

"Oh!" I say brightly. "Where are you off to?"

"Brighton." He sighs.

"What's wrong with Brighton?"

"Nothing, it's just . . . the context. My aunt and uncle—my mum's sister and her husband, they're coming from Italy, and my parents are so weird about them coming to our new place that they've insisted we all meet in Brighton instead."

"Your new place that's exactly like my place?" I say, trying not to roll my eyes.

"Yeah, I mean, obviously I don't think there's anything wrong with it, but my parents are really into this whole thing of keeping up appearances, and for my aunt and uncle to see that they don't live in a big fancy house anymore would be a real killer for them."

“That sucks.”

“So, yeah, Brighton,” he says. “But we’ll be back on it on Monday, yeah?”

“Yeah,” I tell him. “I’m going to be brave and go it alone for my next session.”

“I’ll miss our little afternoon session! I’ll think about you at five thirty on Friday.”

I roll my eyes. “No, you won’t.”

Ollie doesn’t reply. He just frowns and looks uncomfortable.

And speaking of uncomfortable . . . now I’ve got to do the Zoom with Dad. Ugh! I am so extremely not in the mood for this. I wouldn’t be at the best of times, and this is the *worst* of times. I’m a failure.

CHAPTER 21

I shower and change and head downstairs where Jake is propping his laptop up on a stack of big books.

"All right," he says, not looking at me. I can tell he's anxious about this too.

"Yeah."

"Mum's ordered the pizzas. They're coming any minute now."

"OK," I say. "Do you want me to do anything?"

"No, I don't think so. Maybe go get Sash?"

I walk back to the bottom of the stairs and call her name. She appears in her pajamas. "Don't forget we're talking to Dad now, yeah?"

"Oh yeah," she says. Even though she had clearly forgotten, I'm oddly pleased to know it hasn't been hanging over her in the same way it's been hanging over me.

The doorbell rings and Mum answers it. The smell of pizza fills the room, and I go to help her with the boxes. I look at the clock on the living room wall. Only a few minutes until our appointed time. I busy myself by getting out plates and transferring personal pizzas to them (Margherita for Sasha, pepperoni for Jake, and one with salty things on it for me) and taking the plates into the living room, and then it's time, so we all crowd onto the sofa and Mum goes and starts piping the icing onto a birthday cake in the kitchen, spinning the turntable with one hand while she ices with the other. Jake leans over and opens the link Dad sent us, and when we join the Zoom and Jake sits back on the sofa, we're sitting so uncomfortably that it looks like a hostage video but with pizza.

Dad is *always* late for everything. Tonight is no exception, so we just sit in silence for a few minutes, looking at our reflections, contemplating how weird it is for us to all be piled onto one sofa when normally we would be spread out across different seats, but tonight we have to be crowded into the frame so he can see all of us. It feels very unnatural. But then we see Dad's face, and it's so the same and so much the thing we've been seeing all our lives that it makes my chest hurt. Not like when I'm running, not that spiky, scratchy breathing feeling but a way that makes me feel heavy and hollow at the same time. His brown eyes and almost black hair and his beard that's going gray and that softness of his features, like a big puppy or something. That's the face I saw all my life until this summer. That's my dad.

"All right, you horrible lot," he says, smiling broadly when we appear on his screen, exactly the way he would say it when he got home from work.

"Hi, Daddy," says Sasha.

Jake and I don't say anything yet; I'm still too taken aback by seeing him on video rather than in person. Then I remember the whole point of us doing this is so we can talk, so I say, "Hi!" It comes out too bright, too chirpy. It must definitely register as fake, but it's the best I have right now.

Jake just grunts something that could be a *hello* but might just be a grunt, who can say?

"Got your pizzas? From Gino's, yeah?"

"Always," I say, mustering a smile. I hold up my plate to show him my pizza with its anchovies and olives and capers.

"Salty!" he says, screwing up his face in disapproval.

"What you got, Sash? Margherita?" Sasha nods as she eats a slice. "And the one with all the meats on it for you, Jake?"

"No, just pepperoni," he mumbles.

I realize it's going to fall on me to make this work. "Have you found a new pizza place?" I ask.

"I'm working on it. Gem—" he says before stopping himself. *Gemma*. A forbidden word. At least right now. "I've been told that the place I got this is the best one around, but it's not *quite* Gino's. Not bad, though."

"There's no such thing as bad pizza," I say. And then no one says anything. And no one says anything. And no one says anything. "How's—" I begin, but Dad speaks at the same time as me.

"No, you go on, Roo," he says.

"No, it was nothing," I say, shaking my head. "I was just going to ask how your new work is."

"Oh, it's all right, nothing too exciting . . . But I suppose accountancy never has been very exciting, has it?"

"Nope," says Jake flatly. I think of the time Jake complained about Mum not putting Dad on the phone while we were eating dinner. How eager he seemed to talk to him. And now that he's presented with him in person (sort of), it's all fallen apart. Too real. Too much.

"So . . ." Dad says with a sigh. "What are you spending your school holidays doing?"

"Ruby's doing running," says Sasha enthusiastically, which makes me feel a little sparkle somewhere in my chest.

"Is she?" Dad frowns, like Sasha must be mistaken.

"She is," I say, and I expect Jake to jump in with something to make it clear how absurd this proposition is, but he doesn't. That's how you can tell he's really feeling defeated. Not taking an opportunity to make fun of me. "I'm entering the Dawson Dash. I'm going to try to win it," I say.

"Oh!" Dad says, looking bemused. "Good for you!"

"Jake's mostly been hanging around here and working at the pub in the evenings, haven't you?" I go on.

"Yeah," he says.

"Getting good tips?" Dad asks.

"Yeah, not bad," Jake says, looking into the camera as he speaks, which makes a change from the way he's been avoiding digital eye contact with Dad this evening.

Silence. We all pretend our pizzas are very interesting and important and chew away at them with our eyes down. It's a world apart from our Wednesday-night takeaways together.

Then Dad's head jerks to one side and there's a jingle of keys.

"Hiya, darling!" comes a woman's voice, and we see her walk into the sight line of his laptop camera and kiss him on the cheek. And, just like that, the bottom falls out of my stomach. Like I'm in a lift that's dropping ten floors in one go. I feel it in myself and somehow it's like I'm feeling it for Mum who didn't even see it. Oh no. This was not part of the plan. "What are you watching?" She peers at the screen. A face. Lots of long brown hair. Nice makeup. A floral sundress. "Oh!"

"Gemma!" he says almost angrily. "I told you! I told you this was tonight! I thought you were staying out!"

"I forgot!" she says, exasperated. "Is that a crime?"

We sit in the tensest silence imaginable until Jake's voice cuts through, higher and more wobbly than usual. "Is that her?"

"Jake, I . . ." Dad begins, then turns to the woman. "Can you go somewhere else, please? Just while I sort this out."

"All right!" says the woman impatiently before disappearing out of the frame. But there wasn't much point in Dad trying to get rid of her, because Jake leaps forward and slams the laptop shut before slumping back on the sofa and nibbling at his thumbnail with a dark expression.

"Who was that?" Sasha asks. It's clear she already knows what's going on but just wants someone to say it.

"His new girlfriend," I say, sighing. I look over to the kitchen where Mum is standing with an icing bag in her hands, not moving, wondering if she should come in. It's impossible that she didn't hear the whole thing, isn't aware of what happened. I feel a lump in my throat. It's all so real now. Not that it wasn't before, but . . . now it *really* is. He really is somewhere else. He really is living with someone new. It's all really happening, and there's no going back now.

"Mate," I say, putting my arm around Jake, which isn't something I do very often. "Are you OK?" He doesn't answer, just keeps nibbling his thumbnail.

"It's just shit," he says finally. He gets to his feet and goes up to his room, taking the stairs two at a time.

"Yeah," I say softly, even though I know he can't hear me.

Jake's departure prompts Mum to put down the icing bag and come into the living room.

"Can I go to my room now?" Sasha asks her.

"Take your pizza with you," Mum says, sliding into Jake's vacant place on the sofa.

"No, it's OK. I'm done with it."

Mum looks at her, trying to figure out what to say next. "Take one slice with you," she says.

Sasha sighs in her unintentionally funny, theatrical way, which fails to make me laugh right now. "Fine," she says, sliding a slice off the plate and carrying it upstairs with her.

And then it's just me and Mum.

"That was tough," I say.

"It *is* tough, isn't it?" Mum says, biting her lip. Biting at the skin in exactly the same way that I do.

"Mum . . ." I say, my heart feeling heavy and full at the same time.

"Yes, baby?"

"Are you doing OK?"

There's a pause for a second and then she laughs, but it doesn't sound like she means it. It sounds like something she just realized she had to do. "I'm doing fine, Roo. Don't worry about me."

"It's just . . ."

"Just what?"

"I saw you in the front garden a couple of times. In the night."

"Well, then," she says. "It's hard. It's really hard. That's the truth of it, for me as well as for you lot. But it's not for *you* to worry about."

"But I do worry," I say quietly.

"Remember, Roo, I've got lots of friends, and Auntie Siobhan and lots of people to talk to if I'm feeling down about it. It's not something for you to worry about, like I said. Yes, sometimes I have a little meltdown, but that's something I've just got to go through. I don't want you worrying about me." She looks at me and holds her arms out. "You're so good. Such a good girl."

I let her pull me into a hug. "I'm all right." She kisses the top of my head.

Maybe we'll all be all right in the end.

CHAPTER 22

When I meet up with Liv on Monday, I'm half keen to get out running again that evening to prove to myself that I *can* do it, and half all cloudy and anxious at the idea that I literally can't.

Liv sighs. "This is just a temporary blip. It's bad timing," she says as we lean over the railing in Horniman Gardens and try to touch an alpaca. The alpaca does not wish to be touched. We respect its wishes. "Like, your brother was a dick to you. And then you found running hard. Finding running hard is not proof that your brother was right. If anything, it's proof that a lot of this stuff—like, whether you can do it—is kind of . . . in your head?"

"Which is *exactly* what kicked off the beef with my brother in the first place! That very topic!"

"So you were right. You went into that run questioning whether you could do it, whether your body would ever let you do it. Instead of being like, *Hell yeah, of course I can do it, why wouldn't I?* You know?"

I nod. "I mean, there is still a strong chance I literally cannot do it. That I'm not a runner, that I'm not cut out for it."

"I mean, sure! It's not for everyone, and you can obviously give up at any time, but . . . you do kind of like it, right? That sense of satisfaction when you finish, those sweet endorphins?"

"Yeah . . ."

"So! That's all the reason you need to keep going, because you *can* do it. You're already doing it. Anyway, it's not like you're the first cool fat babe to ever wear a sports bra."

"No, there's . . . you," I say, trying to think of others.

Liv takes her phone out of her back pocket and taps at the screen with her thumb, the nail bitten short. She holds up the phone. "Well, there's her," she says, and I squint in the sunshine at the screen where I can make out a cool dark-skinned woman doing a headstand in yoga. She takes the phone back and then presents it to me again with a woman with flowing, glossy hair in a hot-pink Lycra set doing boxercise on a beach. And then someone heavily tattooed lifting weights with a smile. All fat. Warmth spreads through my chest. Comfort, I think it is.

"All fat," Liv says, like she's reading my mind. "And, like you said, there's me. And all of that is even more true than what your brother said to you. Because this is real! These women are real! I'm real! You're real! He's the one who's just making shit up!"

I nod, feeling a smile begin to form. Last time I tried was so rubbish, so demotivating, so all-around *bleh* that I think I really did believe Jake was right.

"Follow them *all*," Liv says. "I command you. It'll be good for you, and in turn it'll help you be good for your sister."

"I will!" And then, wanting to do something good for her in return, I say, "So April was pretty hyped that I had been hanging out with you."

Liv raises an eyebrow. I should ask her how she does that, but now's not the time. "She was?"

"She was. I was thinking you two should meet sometime. Like, I could introduce you in a non-cringe way."

"I would be up for that," Liv says nonchalantly, but I can tell she's into the idea. Ruby Morgan, matchmaker! Is there no end to my skills?

Well, that question is tested when I'm back out with Ollie later in the afternoon. *Can* I do this?

"We're going to try a slightly different route," he says. "We'll start on the other side of the park this time, just so it doesn't feel like you're doing exactly the same thing over again. The other day we fell a little short, but there's no reason why you can't smash it today."

I nod. "I know," I tell him, my face set resolutely.

"That's what I want to hear more of! I kept thinking of you this weekend. I felt so bad, like I'd abandoned you when you needed a boost. But it sounds like you've gotten there all by yourself."

"Well, that remains to be seen, but at least I'm going in with a good attitude."

He looks at his phone, setting the timer. "Just pace yourself. Go as slowly as you need to at first so you can keep your energy up until the end. You don't want to burn out too soon. You ready?"

"You bet."

"Let's go!"

We set off. Slowly, slowly. More slowly than usual. More slowly than before. I know what it feels like to have to run for this long, and I need to be able to see this through. I need to preserve my energy and effort for when I really need it. We run along the long, straight road of fancy houses on the other side of the park, and when we reach the end after a few minutes, my breathing starts to change. I feel it catching in my chest. But I won't let it get the better of me.

As if he can read my mind, Ollie says (because he can talk while he runs, like it's not even a thing), "Take long breaths through your nose and then breathe out slowly. Try to just focus on that for now."

I nod, not wanting to waste any of my precious energy on talking.

In. Slowly. Out. Slowly. In. Slowly. Out. Slowly. I feel the number of times my feet hit the pavement increase between each breath. I feel my body complying more and more. I just need to keep doing this: keep it up, not stop. I just need to not stop. And I don't stop, not yet. I keep going as Ollie leads me down through Mayow Park and around the outer path and back out of the farther gate on the same side again. Running up the slight incline on the road outside the park feels like climbing Everest, but I do it. I keep going. I keep going because I can. Because I know I can.

"We're halfway done!" Ollie says, and part of me can't believe we have to do this all over again, that I'm barely on the other side of the mountain, but a louder part of me says, *Of course you can do this again*. So I follow him along the road where we started the other day, but running in the opposite direction, and I think of how sure I was that I simply couldn't do it and how much I regretted proving myself right, and I power through until we get to the end of the road and turn right on Dacres Road and I'm sure I can hear a woodpecker in the nature reserve and how cool is that and I wouldn't be hearing that if I was at home right now and yes! On the other side of this block of flats is the downward slope! Sweet relief floods my aching calves as we head downhill, which means that by the time we turn off to run all the way along Inglemere

Road, my body feels ready for it after that little rest. My body feels ready for it! Even though it hurts and my breathing is really not playing ball right now, I'm still going! I've walked along this road hundreds of times in my life, and it's only from running back along it now that I've noticed it's not flat—it's on a slope. I feel every degree of this slope as I push on, running just behind Ollie. The modernist church at the end of the road seems so far away, but I will get there if I just keep putting one foot in front of the other. In fact, it's impossible that I *won't* get there as long as I just keep going. So I do, and when we get back to the downward slope of Dacres Road and turn right to continue our downhill trajectory, I feel so grateful to myself that I've just run up and down Inglemere Road since I was last here on this corner. I feel grateful and happy and so completely determined to see this through because I know I can. We run past the house with the life-size cuddly polar bear in the window, past the flats where the front garden is blanketed in crocuses in the springtime, on and on until—

"Stop!" Ollie says. "You did it!"

I stand, doubled over from the sheer effort of not giving up, of telling my body I could do it because my brain knew I could. My chest feels like it's full of metal, jangling around in my lungs. But I feel such a rush, a lightness there too. Is this what they call . . . endorphins?

"Keep walking! Don't stand still for too long!" Ollie tells me, and I grudgingly pick up the pace again.

"I . . . did . . . it . . ." I pant. I wonder how far off the five kilometers of the Dawson Dash this was. How far am I off my goal?

"You did! You knew you could! I knew you could!" he says, grinning.

This feels about a thousand million times better than last

Wednesday felt. I couldn't do it last week because I literally *couldn't* do it then. My brain was not in the right place. I felt all wrong, disheartened, downbeat. And that meant I couldn't do it. But today was the right time. I felt motivated and inspired and determined and so I *could* do it. I smashed it!

I mean, I can barely haul myself up the stairs over the railway bridge back to home, but I did it. My legs are shaking so much as I try to walk down the other side that I have to go slow like a snail.

Ollie looks back up at me from several steps ahead. "Want a hand?" he offers.

"No, that's OK," I say.

"Sure?" he says, holding out his hand toward me. I don't want him touching my sweaty palm at a time like this! No way!

I nod and continue my slow descent.

"You really are making great progress, you know," he says on the short stretch between the bridge and home.

"I know. I mean, I know that now. I was talking such a big game in the beginning, but I didn't really believe it. And then I *really* didn't believe it when I actually started running. But now . . . maybe I do? Liv gave me such an amazing pep talk and showed me all these cool plus-size exercise babes and it just made me feel like, *Yeah, this is within my capabilities*, you know?"

Ollie nods thoughtfully, like he's trying to figure something out. "So from now we'll just be adding more and more time until the race. Which is . . ."

"In, like, three weeks," I say, my stomach knotting itself up at the thought.

"Well," he says, shrugging, "if you bring the kind of vibe you had today, then there's no reason why you won't be totally ready in the next three weeks."

I clap my hands together. "Between you and Liv, I've got all the pep talks I could possibly need."

"You two are getting pretty close," he says, glancing at me, like he's trying to read my expression.

"Yeah, she's cool. Like, really cool," I say, trying to figure out what he wants me to say.

"Oh, by the way, don't forget to register. They sent the sign-up link to our school email addresses the other day."

"I barely even knew we had a school email address . . . I don't know if I even remember my password," I say, trying to cast my mind back to whatever day, many moons ago, when I had to set it. What password would my brain have settled for on that particular day?

Ollie smiles. "It helps that I only got my password at the beginning of the summer holidays, I guess. You want me to do your registration for you when I do mine?"

I look up at him, embarrassed at my own uselessness. "Yes, please."

"No problem. I'll sign you up. That way you *can't* back out."

"I literally can, though. I could just not turn up."

"No way," he says, shaking his head. "I feel like you're the kind of girl who if you say you're going to do something, you do it."

I blush. "I guess I am . . ."

We're approaching our houses, and I feel so high and light and full of love for all the world that I don't want Ollie to go.

"Oh, wait a second!" he says, holding up a finger. "Wait there." He dashes to his front door and lets himself in, leaving the door ajar. He emerges a minute later with a small square cardboard box tied with a red ribbon. What is it?

As he passes it to me, my hand brushes against his, and it's soft and warm and I want to take hold of it. I pull the ribbon off the box and open it, and inside are heart-shaped cookies piped with icing and an elegant *R* in the middle. I feel all the blood rush to my cheeks. I just stare at them, my heart beating hard in my chest. He's looking at me very tentatively as if I might laugh in his face or have to let him down gently.

"I want to do more fancy icing because I think that might be something I could kind of . . . specialize in once I get properly started, and I wanted to practice. I told my dad it was your birthday and I needed to make them for you, so he didn't grill me on why I'm trying to get good at this stuff," he says, smiling sadly.

"But it's not . . ." I say stupidly.

"No," he says, blushing. "I just felt like making them." A pause. "For you."

Is this . . . real? Did Ollie, my actual crush, make actual heart-shaped cookies for me, just because? Is this a thing that happens to me? We stare at each other. His eyes look so big and expectant. I don't know what to do exactly. I don't know if this is enough evidence that he could possibly, maybe, be a tiny, tiny, small bit interested in me, or if I should wait and see.

"Well," I say, swallowing hard, "thank you." Infused with the confidence of hanging out with Liv and smashing our run today and this random act of kindness, I decide to be very brave. "I was wondering if you wanted to hang out sometime . . . away from the whole running thing?"

He smiles. "Yeah. Let's."

"How about . . . tomorrow? Since we're not running. Or is that too soon?" I say quickly.

"No, tomorrow is good. Your mum texted me to say the local delivery would be shorter tomorrow, so we could hang out after that when I'm back?"

"I can't believe my mum texts you," I say, face-palming, but mostly basking in the delicious glow of Ollie making plans with me.

"You can text me if you want." He doesn't look at me, just at his right foot, which is drawing a circle on the pavement.

"I don't have your number," I say, and I can't help but smile.

"Give me yours," he says, knowing I don't bring my phone out when we go running. I tell him mine and he puts it into his phone. "So tomorrow evening, yeah? We can go somewhere when I'm back."

"It's a . . ." I say, before catching myself. It might *not* be a date. "I'll see you then."

"See you then," he says, and heads back into his house, leaving me holding the box. I stare at it and wonder how things got so good.

CHAPTER 23

Hanging! Out! With! Ollie! Day! Nothing can get in the way of my good mood today, I tell you! No, of course I don't *really* expect anything to happen this evening, but a girl can dream, can't she? I do a little bit of makeup. Nothing too extravagant, nothing that would require Salma's skills, but, you know, something a little bit more seductive than sweaty and puce like he normally sees me. What a day!

Can you give me a ring when you have a minute?

Oh. Classic. Something to burst my good-vibes balloon. A text from Dad. I have a minute now. I suppose I could call him. We haven't really spoken since the cursed Zoom call the other day. That was nearly a week ago now. A couple of texts, but nothing proper. I take a deep breath and press the little phone icon next to his name at the top of the screen.

It barely rings before he answers. "Hello, Roo," he says. "You all right?"

"I'm OK," I say. "How are you?"

"Better for hearing your voice," he says.

I don't say anything yet. I don't know what to say. And anyway, he's the one who wanted to talk.

"So . . . Wednesday evening didn't really go to plan, did it?"

"Not really."

"I just wanted to say . . . I'm sorry about that. It's not what I had in mind."

I stay silent, unsure if he has more to say or if I'm expected to say something now.

"That's OK," I say finally.

"I know it can't be easy on you lot . . ."

"No," I say, swallowing down the lump in my throat. "At first I thought it was mostly Jake, but it's hard for me too. Maybe even Sasha, but she seems all right."

"This summer has been . . ." He pauses. "Well, it's been horrible without you. And it's been even more horrible with this lack of contact we've been having."

"I know . . . I know . . ." I say. "I know that I shouldn't be so . . ."

"No, it's not your fault," Dad says emphatically. "I made this mess. And if you need some time to deal with it in your own way, that's OK with me. But I really miss you, that's all. I don't know what I was expecting with all this . . ."

"Yeah," I say sadly. I don't know what he was expecting either. Leaving his family to move to a new city to be with a woman he'd been cheating on his wife with for six months? You don't have to be a genius like me to see that's a bad call. But hey ho.

"To tell you the truth," he says, and even though I can't *actually* see him, I feel like I can see him raking his hands through the back of his hair like he always does when he's considering something with great seriousness, "I don't know if it's really been worth it."

"Mmmm," I say.

It's not like Mum didn't try to tell him that about a thousand times, but by then their relationship was already so badly broken that they couldn't have stayed together anyway. But still, he didn't need to actually *move in with her.*

"Sorry, you don't need me to tell you all this."

"It's OK. It's good to know, I guess," I say, even though knowing that it might not have even been worth all the pain is somehow much, much worse than knowing he feels like it was.

"I just wanted to say sorry for the other night, really."

"I think it was just hard for us to, like, *see* you there. Even without, you know, the interruption. It really felt different for me, I guess? And I think it was the same for Jake too."

"I know," he says. "I know." We sit in silence, miles apart. "We'll get through this. I just wanted to tell you that I love you and I'm sorry for all the mess I've made this year. We *will* get through it," he says again.

"I know," I say, because it's true—I know we will. This is just the shit part. The worst part. And we just have to live through this first. "I love you too."

"Good. Well, I'm at work so I'd better go back to my desk, but I just kept thinking about you since last week and I wanted to talk to you. I love you," he says again.

And again I say, "I love you too. Bye, Dad."

"Bye, Roo."

And when we hang up, nothing has really changed, but it means something to me that he's not just off living some dream life without us. That it does hurt him, and it isn't just hurting us.

I try to revive that peppy feeling of having a non-date with Ollie on my horizon and start rummaging through my wardrobe for something cute to wear. As I'm mid-change, a ribbed vest top halfway over my head, I hear my bedroom door open, and by the time I've got the vest off, Sasha is already flopped on my bed.

"Ever heard of knocking?"

She shrugs, looking at me with interest. "What are you doing?"

"I'm making a mess, that's what I'm doing."

"Are you going out?"

"Yes, I'm going to meet someone."

"What are you going to do?"

"I don't know yet."

"A girl or a boy?"

"A boy."

"Oh." I wonder why she's in here.

I stand in my underwear, looking at my wardrobe, or what's left in it now that most of it is on my bed.

Sasha's still eyeing me, now with even more intensity for a ten-year-old. "Roo," she says, frowning and sitting up straight like she wants to be taken very seriously.

"Yes?" I say, hoping she gets to the point soon because I'm just about ready to go out, but also wanting to be infinitely patient with her.

"Do you ever wish you looked different?"

Part of me wants to stall for time, disingenuously ask, *Different like how?* But I know what she means. I know what she's asking. And I could tell her the truth or I could lie. I could shrug and say *Sometimes*, because it's true, because I get sick of being treated like I'm some alien anomaly by boys or by my brother or when I turn on the TV or read a book. Or I could say *No*, because it's not like it never crosses my mind, but it *feels* more like the truth because it's what I feel—me, Ruby.

"No," I say, which is a lie. "I like the way I look." Which is a truth. Let's do the broad strokes now and get to the nuances later, when she's not, you know, literally ten years old.

"Oh," she says. I can't read her tone, whether it's surprise or skepticism or happiness.

"Why do you ask?"

She shrugs.

I'm tempted to leave it there, not least because I'm on a deadline. But I just can't. "Do you?"

"I wish I looked more like everyone else at school," she says simply. "I wish I didn't look different."

I think for a second, wondering how to approach this. "But . . ." I say, wanting to get it right. I think of Liv. I think of how right she made it all feel to me. "Mason has green eyes and really pale skin, and Charlotte has freckles and ginger hair, and Femi is taller than everyone else and he's Black, and Ellie has a gap between her front teeth, and Archana has the longest hair I've ever seen. It's not like *everyone else* looks the same, is it?"

She moves her lips against her teeth. "No . . . But they're not . . ."

"Not chubby?" I offer her.

She nods.

I shrug. "That's just *your* variation. None of us are the same. We *all* have stuff that makes us different, and none of that stuff is bad. At least, I don't think so." I start pulling on clothes. "I mean . . . I know I would like to believe I do, but I actually don't know everything. So I can only really tell you what I think. But that's what I think. And I don't think there's anything wrong with me, and I don't think there's anything wrong with you either." I sit on the bed to lace up my trainers.

"I'll think about it," she says resolutely, like whether to continue worrying about her body is a decision she has to make. And maybe it is.

"Don't think too much. You're meant to be having fun," I say, springing up from the bed. "Now, I've got to go out, and I'm not having you in here snooping around while I'm not home."

"I don't snoop!" Her exasperated tone makes her sound like a weary middle-aged woman, not a cherubic ten-year-old.

"Yeah, yeah . . ." I say, pulling her ponytail as she graciously follows my instructions to return to her own room with her own things in it.

Just then, there's an urgent rapping on the door. I check the time on my phone and see it's later than I thought it was. Ollie's been taking his time. But why so impatient?

I pull open the door.

"Oh!" I say, when I'm faced with Ollie's mum.

"Hi, Ruby, is it?" She doesn't wait for me to answer. "Oliver said you were the Ruby from when he was little, but I'm not sure I would have recognized you after all this time," she says quickly, her brow furrowed. "I'm Oliver's mum—I was wondering if you knew where Oliver was? Have you seen him?"

I swallow. I do know where he is. He's out delivering for Mum. "Ummm . . ." I say, stalling for time.

"It's just I've been trying to get ahold of him for a while, and he wasn't answering his phone, and now it's going straight to voicemail," she says, her voice rising with panic.

"And that's not normal for him?" I ask, because I actually don't know.

"No, it's not," she says impatiently before bringing a hand to her forehead. "I wouldn't normally worry so much, but I just saw a cyclist had been hit outside Sainsbury's and the bike looked like Oliver's and now I've gotten myself all worked up because I can't get ahold of him."

Now it's my turn to panic. My heart starts thudding in my chest. I feel lightheaded. Could it be him? It couldn't be, could it? But . . . it has to be someone. What am I meant to do? Should I tell her? I have to tell her, don't I?

"Well, actually . . ." I say, because I can't stand us looking at each other wordlessly any longer. "I do sort of know where he is."

"Yes?" she says, eyes wide.

"He's out doing deliveries for my mum, for her baking business. He's out on his bike." As soon as the words leave my mouth, I'm swamped with regret. But if he's really in trouble, then it'll be worth it, right? Surely this is an extreme situation; surely I'm justified?

"He's doing what? While I'm out at work?"

"My mum runs a baking business . . . and she needed someone to do local deliveries . . . and Ollie said he would do it on his bike so he could make a bit of money . . . and it's Tuesdays he does his deliveries. Tuesday afternoons. So that's . . . well, that's where he is now."

"On his bike . . ." Her face is pure panic. "Why wouldn't he tell us? Why is he hiding things from us?" I can't tell if she's asking me or if she's asking herself.

"Well . . ." I venture, "I think he thought you were, you know, so against him taking this all seriously, you know, baking and that kind of stuff . . . so maybe that's why . . ."

She shakes her head. "My God, this is all so stupid, pushing him away like this! This is what happens when you don't let your children be themselves!"

I don't know what to say to calm her nerves, and I realize that now I'm scared too.

"I have to go," she says. "I'll go back to Sainsbury's and make sure it's not him. Oh God, oh God . . ."

"OK," I say, nodding. "I'm sure it's not him . . ." But she's already hurrying down the path and out of the gate, which stands swinging in her wake.

I flop on the sofa, stomach churning. Only a few minutes ago I had nothing to worry about but my non-running hangout with Ollie tonight, and now I'm like . . . is he . . . you know . . . dead? And if he's not, I've just bloody blurted out the thing he asked me to keep quiet about!

I nibble at the skin on my lip as I lie on the sofa. I wish Mum was home, not out for coffee with her mate Tara. At least Jake isn't here to make things worse like he inevitably would. Should I have gone looking for Ollie with her? It didn't seem like she wanted me to, but now I'm just lying here, useless. I wish I had something to do. What should I do?

The doorbell jolts me out of my anxiety spiral. I jump to my feet and dash to the door.

Ollie smiles as I open it. "You look nice." Ollie! "God, what a terrible time *that* was."

"Oh my God, you're alive!" I say, not even able to enjoy the compliment.

"Yeeees?" he says, tilting his head inquisitively. He bends down to unclip the trailer from the bike, looking up at me for further elaboration. "I wasn't dead. I was just having bike trouble. My chain broke and I had to walk it back from the last drop-off. Luckily that was only over by Wells Park, but it really slowed me down, and my phone had run out of batteries from me checking the map so often, so I couldn't even listen to music as I was pushing this piece of junk home. I *always* charge my phone before I go out delivering, but today I didn't and look where it got me." He stands back up, shrugging his shoulders in that lovely loose way he has.

"Ollie . . . shit . . ."

"What's the matter?"

"I did something bad," I say, returning to the bit of skin on my lip I had been nibbling. "Your mum came around not that long ago."

"Why? What's wrong? She was calling me while I was cycling and I was going to ring her back, but then my phone died." He frowns at me.

"No, there's nothing wrong now that you're back . . . She couldn't get ahold of you and she'd seen an accident on the main road outside Sainsbury's, a cyclist, with a bike that looked like yours, and she got it into her head that it was you and, to be honest, I did too, so I told her that you were out on your bike."

"Shit," he says, his face falling. "Did you tell her it was for your mum?"

I nod.

"Shit," he says again.

"Maybe she'll be so relieved you're not dead that she won't mind you've been doing stuff for my mum?"

He shakes his head. "No, it'll become a way bigger thing because I've been lying to them. I just didn't want to have to have a whole conversation about my *future* and my *prospects*, but now that I've been doing this for weeks, it's turned into a whole thing. Shit . . . was there really no way you couldn't tell her?"

"No!" I say indignantly. "She was so worried! You need to call her right now."

"Fine," he says, leaving the trailer on the ground and hopping over the wall to his house. When his front door closes behind him, it hits me.

We're not going to be hanging out tonight.

CHAPTER 24

One day later, I put on my kit. I'm ready to go out again. Ready to run for longer—maybe twenty-five minutes this time. I can do it, I can do it, I can do it. I can't let this weird thing with Ollie get in my way. But maybe *he* can. I have no idea when I go downstairs whether he'll be outside, waiting for me, because it's our usual time and place. I don't dare look out the window to check because I don't want to see he's not there. When I turn the door handle and call out to Mum that I'm going running, I see that my hand is shaking. Please let him be there, so I don't have to wait and don't have to wonder. Please let everything be OK! That's all I ask! I pull the door toward me and . . .

Nothing. He's not there. I feel the pit of my stomach hollow out. I sit on the wall and wait for him, and I'm so caught up in my thoughts about Ollie, and me, and Ollie and me and how close it felt like we were getting to *something* that it takes me a few minutes to even notice that his house is dark. There's no movement inside. No TV on. Nothing. Blank. Empty. That's . . . weird. I hop over the wall and ring the doorbell. I hear it trill inside the house. I realize that if there were signs of life in there, I wouldn't have rang it. I would have been too self-conscious about a personalized rejection by Ollie. It's just to confirm to myself that there really is no one there. Is he . . . avoiding me? He could just tell me he doesn't want to run with me today. Or next time. Or however long it'll take for him to cool off.

Wondering where he is won't help me get ready for the Dash. If he wanted to be here, he would be here. Plus, he has my phone number now, so he clearly didn't *want* to let me know he wouldn't be around. I've just got to do it on my own. And now that I've cleared that hurdle of going for twenty minutes nonstop, I'm feeling like nothing can stand in my way. With or without Ollie, I know I can see this through. I run back inside to pick up my phone to time myself and, if I'm honest, check to see if he's texted me. He hasn't.

And then I set out. Straight from my door. I just go, along streets around my house, feeling my legs get heavier and my breathing get harder. I keep checking the time on the stopwatch thing on my phone, and it feels like time isn't moving forward at all, so I decide I won't check it again and just try to zone out. Zone out, zone out, zone out. Come on, Ruby, stop thinking about how much longer you have to run. What shall I think about instead? Ollie? Well, that was a nice thing to think about before and now it's just a horrible thing to think about. A missed opportunity. He doesn't even want to talk to me. Is he really properly avoiding me? Or am I just being silly and arrogant? This isn't a good distraction. Ow! What's that? A stitch—I've got a stitch? Is this a joke? This is the last thing I need. Should I slow down? Should I stop? I don't *want* to stop, though. For all my griping, I feel like I can keep going. But this hurts! I try to control my breathing. I figure everything seems to always be about breathing. I slow down, but I don't stop. I make sure my breaths are r e a l l y l o n g, deep, and controlled. And eventually it goes away. See! I didn't need to stop! Take that, body! Hmm, what shall I think about now that I've saved myself from death by stitch? I think about Liv and wonder if it's too soon to suggest we hang out again or if that would be too *keen*. I want to be true to my word and see if I can fix her up with April. But also . . . I love hanging out with her! She makes me feel like maybe I'm not completely wrong about everything. She's the nice little counterbalance to all the poisonous shit my brother spouts.

Trot, trot, trot, I go, just determined, focused. *In the zone.* I'm in the zone. I'm running. I'm still running. Oh, that's a cute little dog that I'm trotting toward! So fluffy! Like a little cloud! No, wait, isn't that Mr. Pearce's dog, and isn't that Mr. Pearce *with* the dog? Ugh! Him again! Him of the Round Hill fat-shaming! I thought I'd seen the last of him!

I narrow my eyes and put on my game face. He's walking ahead of me on the pavement. Against my usual relaxed nature, I decide to speed up. I do something I haven't done since my first ill-advised puke run and break into a sprint. *THUNK! THUNK! THUNK!* go my feet on the pavement (as opposed to the usual *thunk! thunk! thunk!*). *WHAT ARE YOU DOING?!* go my lungs. As I zoom past Mr. Pearce at great speed, I call over my shoulder to him, "Hurry up, slowpoke!" before disappearing around the corner onto Carlton Terrace where I nearly collapse into a heap from the effort of the sprint, but I don't! I keep going! Take that, Mr. Pearce!

When my phone finally beeps its piercing little alarm, I nearly jump out of my skin. I'm done?! I did it! I can barely breathe and I'm covered in sweat, but . . . I did it! I'm building! And I did it on my own! Did I *like* doing it on my own? Not really, but I did it! Now . . . where am I? I open my maps app and figure out a route home. I should probably have been more strategic with where I went, because now I'm somewhere on the other side of the railway line. If I'd been smart, I would have done a circular thing, wouldn't I? Lots to learn.

As I make my way home, panting and sweating in my trademark Ruby fashion, I text Liv while the adrenaline and endorphins are doing their thing.

Fancy coming for a run with me sometime?

Hmmm . . . it wouldn't be my FAVORITE way to hang out. I'm not much of a runner.

It'll be fun because it's with me.

I don't think I've ever voluntarily gone for a run with another person.

No pressure!

Fine, you've twisted my arm. Where do you go?

Mayow Park, Wells Park, sometimes Crystal Palace.

Change of scenery then? Dulwich Park?

Let's do it!

Sunday 11am OK with you? That entrance before the horse school. You know where I mean, yeah?

That was easy enough. I've never run on a weekend before. Or in the morning for that matter. It'll be like looking into some unknown world, seeing how other people do things. Amid my elation at completing a twenty-five-minute run—yes, a *whole* five minutes longer than I ran last time—I realize I haven't thought about Ollie in, oh, maybe half an hour. I can't help but wonder where he is, what he's up to, whether he's still angry at me for telling his mum.

I yank my front door key out of the weird little pocket in my leggings and let myself in.

"Oh! There you are," says Mum from the kitchen. "Ollie texted me to say he and his mum and dad have had to go to Italy because his grandad died. He wanted to let me know he wouldn't be able to do deliveries next week and wasn't sure when they would be coming back. He said to tell you he wouldn't be around for a while for your runs."

I swallow. That makes sense. "Did he say anything else?" I ask, not really knowing what I'm wanting to hear.

"Like what?" she says, frowning at me.

I shrug. "I don't know."

"Good on you for going out anyway," she says.

"I'm determined. I've got to see it through. Show Jake who's boss and all that," I tell her.

She looks thoughtful. "I think if it was just about proving Jake wrong you would have given up on it by now."

"What do you mean?" I ask before leaning over the sink to drink from the tap like a cat.

"Can't you use a glass like a normal person?" She sighs, opening the cupboard and handing me one. "Anyway, I mean, you must be enjoying it a bit, yeah? As well as this ridiculous rivalry you two have."

I can't help but smile. "Yeah . . . you know what, I am enjoying it. I didn't think I would . . . But I am."

"I'm glad."

"Makes me kind of annoyed that the way we do PE at school set me up to hate it. Like . . . I felt this was for other people."

Mum smiles. "Well, good on you for changing the story."

I shower, and while I'm under the hot jets, I hope Ollie's texting me. I know he sent a message through my mum, but . . . he could contact me too, right? I did give him my number the other day for this very reason! I nervously poke at the screen when I go back into my bedroom. No text. Bleurgh.

Over dinner I have to listen to Jake going on about some torturous-sounding piece of exercise equipment he wants to buy that Mum says we don't have room for. When he's mid-argument about why it's absolutely, completely essential for his rowing training, my phone illuminates on the dining table. I pick it up. Gasp! It's a text from Ollie.

> Hey, sorry about missing today. Guess your mum said. Not sure when I'll be back.

That's it. Well, it was fun while it lasted, I guess.

CHAPTER 25

The adrenaline rush of doing what I couldn't do only days before definitely gave me a little lift, but underneath it all, I can't help but feel down about Ollie. But I can't wallow. I simply don't have time. The race is *soon*. Like, only a couple of weeks away, and as pumped as I am about the progress I'm making, I know I've still got a long way to go before I'm able to take on the big challenge of the Dawson Dash.

On Saturday evening, the girls and I are basking in the evening sun in Horniman Gardens.

"Best seats in the house!" Jessica says as we stretch out on the patch of grass that faces toward central London, with the Shard piercing the pink evening sky.

"I literally screamed when I saw how many views your video of Jess got," I say to Salma. "You are truly killing it!"

"Thank you! It's all the natural-born talent I have and don't have to work at it at all," she says, winking at me over her can of Cherry Coke. "But, yeah, I was super hyped with how that one went down. Loads of comments about how hot Jess is, naturally."

"Naturally," Jessica says, leaning back on her hands and pouting at us over her shoulder.

"Any from . . . Joshua?" April asks, raising her eyebrows.

"Naturally," Jessica says again in exactly the same tone. "Since he *is* my boyfriend."

We all scream in unison.

"Since when?!" I ask.

She shrugs. "Last week. I wanted to see how it was going, scope him out first before I made a formal announcement."

"Well, I love this for you," April says.

"He's hot," says Jess, "but I'm not sure if he's, like, The One. He asks me a lot of stupid questions, like does the full moon go straight to being a tiny sliver the next day. I don't think he's a match for my huge brain, you know? But for now he's hot enough that I don't care."

"Completely reasonable. Personally I would never compromise in such a way, but I accept the beautiful variety of humanity's rich tapestry," says April, bringing her hands together in serene prayer and closing her eyes.

"What's going on with your running guy? I feel like you never mention him." Jess frowns at me.

I guess I don't, probably because there's never anything to say. It's not like there's any chance I'm going to get with him, *especially* not now.

"Meh," I say.

"Elaborate," Salma demands.

"I was just happy kind of . . . getting to know him, doing this running with him so I don't completely embarrass myself at the Dawson Dash, all of that. And *obviously* I fancy him, but there was no way that was going to happen, right?"

"Wrong," says April impatiently.

"Well, anyway. Then there was this one day this week where I started to actually believe that maaaaaybe something was possible, like it wasn't totally out of the question, you know? It just felt like we'd built up to this point where there was something extra there."

"Like what?" Jess asks, rearranging herself on the grass to face me.

"He loves baking—" I begin.

"Hot," Jess interjects.

"Right?! Anyway, he made me these heart-shaped cookies with my initial on them and this fancy icing around them, and then we made a plan to hang out in a non-running setting."

"Like a date?" Salma says. "Oh my days, tell us about the date!"

I sigh, wishing I did have something to tell them, rather than a whole lot of nothing. "There was no date. I got embroiled in this family beef of his by accident, so the date was off."

"Shit," says Jess. April's just looking at me sadly.

"Shit indeed."

"So what happened when you went running again?" Jess asks.

I throw my hands up. "I don't know! I haven't been running again with him!"

"The beef was *that* bad?" Salma asks, wide-eyed.

"No, it's a whole other thing. He's had to go to Italy because his grandad died, so I haven't seen him since then."

"Shit," Jess says again.

"But there's still hope, yeah?"

I'm both grateful for and annoyed by Salma's optimism. No! There is no hope! I had a chance and it's gone!

"I don't think so. I have no idea when he's coming back, and he just sent me, like, one text to say sorry for missing our run and that he wouldn't be around for a while."

"He's clearly got a lot going on," says April, because she is a rational human being.

"Yeah, of course, but just in terms of anything happening between us . . . I think it was a long shot to begin with and it's definitely off the cards now," I say, trying not to sound too self-pitying, even though I feel extremely self-pitying.

"Why was it a long shot?" Jess asks.

I can't help but wonder if she's being serious or if she's just trying to be a good friend. Surely she's noticed that I've basically gone out of my way to avoid getting into stuff with boys?

"Because . . ." And I realize in that moment that as much as I love my friends, I just don't want to talk about this with them *in particular*. They can love me with all their heart, and I totally believe they do, but there's some stuff that just doesn't feel useful to bring up with them. Like, not only does it not help me, it makes me feel even more distant from them to try to talk about it. And that's OK. I don't need to be able to talk about everything with everyone. Especially now that I have Liv. "Because nothing," I say finally. "Anyway, I've got to focus all my romantic energies into hooking up April and Liv!"

"Tall Liv, the one who plays field hockey?" Jess asks.

"How many are there?" April says, blushing furiously.

"Not that I want to bring up Ollie again, *but* I think he maybe thinks I'm the one who's into Liv because I talk about her so much! But she's just so cool!"

April sighs. "She *is* cool."

As the spotlight shifts to the topic of April and Liv, I can't help but feel grateful that I'm seeing Liv the next day for our run. It's not even like I have anything in particular that I need her advice on, it's just that soothing feeling of being with someone whose brain works the same way as yours.

CHAPTER 26

"Gotta go!" I shout to Mum in the morning as I shove my feet into my trainers, hopping on one foot as I try to do the laces without sitting down. I'm busy! I've got places to be!

"Where are you off to?"

"Going to Dulwich Park with my friend Liv," I say.

"Oh! You don't usually do your running on a weekend," she says over the sound of the stand mixer making buttercream.

"Things have changed! I'm in a glorious new era now—get with the times, Mum," I tell her in a voice of faux exasperation.

"All right, well, have fun!"

It's a longer walk to Dulwich Park than to my normal running haunts and . . . I've got to be honest, I'm running a bit late. Pardon the pun. I've got to get a move on, and there's only one thing for it. Round Hill. My geographic nemesis. We meet again. By the time I make it to run with Liv, I'll have already done the equivalent of a marathon by getting up this slope. I take a deep breath at the bottom and start my stomp up to the top. I feel my calf muscles activate, my bum muscles activate, powering me up, up, up the hill, stomping in my running trainers until I reach the top. I've reached the top? I've reached the top! Suck it, Mr. Pearce! My bum is no smaller, my tummy is no flatter . . . and yet, here I am! On top of Round Hill! Without keeling over or needing to cling on to a postbox for dear life! I do a celebratory jig around the postbox before dashing off down the other side to meet Liv. No more jigs. I don't want to be late.

Liv is leaning against the railings, looking extremely cool in a black sports bra and super-tight black leggings. "Hey," she says as I approach. I let my eyes skim over the roll of fat between the bottom of the sports bra and the top of the leggings, and something about how extremely unapologetic it is makes my heart feel warm.

"I like your athleisure look," I say.

"Thanks. I got sick of the feeling of a T-shirt flapping around me, you know? So you ready for this? How long do you want to go for?"

"I just gave myself a huge warm-up on the way here, so, yes, definitely ready. And . . . shall we do twenty-five minutes?"

"Mate, I'm nervous. Twenty-five? I told you, I'm a short-distance kind of gal."

"How bad can it be? It's just us, right?"

I set a countdown on my phone. I look at her, and she nods at me. "Let's go!" I say, trying to channel Ollie's boundless enthusiasm for the start of a run.

We set off down the entry path. When the path forks, Liv looks at me, like, *Which way?* And I realize that this is my thing. I can decide which way we're going to run. I take us off to the left, and we follow the path around. As we run, I look at Liv's body. *Is this what I look like when I run?* is my first thought. But the more I look at her, the less recognizing my body in hers feels confrontational. It's more . . . comforting. We plod around the park, past the café with its crowds of parents with strollers drinking coffee, through the leafy bits in the middle, and back to where we started. We head up the other side of the park, and maybe it's something about having returned to where we began but not having finished yet that means I start to really feel it. That can't-be-bothered state of mind sets in, even though I've been doing so well today, pushing on, trying my best.

"Let's pep talk each other," I say breathlessly.

"All right, you go first," Liv says, grinning even though she's struggling herself.

"I know you think you can only run short distances . . ." I wheeze. "But I think running longer distances is not that different. It's just your brain standing in the way."

"Not the worst pep talk I've ever heard," she concedes.

"Now do me . . . I feel like I'm flagging a bit," I admit.

"You can give up now if you want to, but I think you can do what you set out to do," she says, only slightly less breathlessly than me.

I nod. She's right. I press on. Even though it's a challenge, I keep putting one foot in front of the other, knowing that I'm already doing more than I ever thought I could do. More than anyone ever told me I was able to do in the body I have.

And then it's done. My phone beeps and we slow our pace and just stand there, grinning. While we're both trying to get our breath back, Liv fixes me with a stare. "Say *thank you*," she says.

Is she all right? I mean, it's not like I made her trek across the Sahara with me.

"Thank . . . you?" I say uncomfortably, wondering if I dragged her away from something important she had to do today.

She hits me gently on the arm with the back of her hand. "Not me, doofus. You. Say thank you to you."

"Oh!" I say. "Thank you, Ruby."

"Your body just did that for you! With you! How cool is that?"

"I suppose it's quite cool . . ." I mumble. "You'll do the race, right?"

"Nah," Liv says, shaking her head. "It's not my vibe. Altogether too much running for me. But I'll be there to cheer you on, I promise."

"You sure you don't want to?"

"Positive. I don't want to run that far, let alone in front of a load of people. If it was a cheeky little sprint, I might be up for it. But I can't be doing with all that distance."

On the one hand, I feel bad about dragging Liv out to do an activity she isn't actually into, but on the other, I can tell she enjoys hanging out as much as I do.

"I'm serious about cheering you on, by the way," she says. "I'll be strategic and position myself somewhere along the route where I think you'll be the most in need of a pep talk yelled at you from the sidelines."

I smile, my breathing feeling more normal again now. Funny how that happens—it's coming back to me quicker and quicker these days, like my body finally understands what it needs to do to help me out. "Thank you in advance."

"It's over there they do it, right?" She nods toward the huge rolling playing fields of St. Alfred's, Ollie's fancy old school. She bends over for a moment, resting her hands on her knees to catch her breath.

"Yeah," I say. "They're so very *charitable* to let us use their grounds one day every year."

"How kind," she says, taking a deep gulp from her water bottle. "So do you feel like you're nearly ready?"

"Kind of yes and kind of no?" I say, wincing. "I think once I've run for half an hour I'll feel like I'm there, you know?"

"You could try that next time. And if you aren't there yet, you've still got time to get there." She makes it sound so manageable, so clear that this is something I can do. Reminds me a bit of Ollie in that way. "So . . . you want to go home or you want to get an iced coffee or something?"

I'm all sweaty and disgusting, but I want to hang out with Liv so much that I don't let it bother me that my hair's all matted and my cheeks are bright pink. I just enjoy our walk to Forest Hill and I enjoy sipping on our ice-cold drinks and I enjoy chatting to her about clothes and bodies and Internet babes to follow and what we want to do after school and it strikes me that maybe it isn't so important if I'm not perfectly put together to hang out with someone that I think is cool . . . Maybe it's OK to let myself be a bit messy and we'll still have fun.

When I hug Liv goodbye and walk home, I just wish I knew I could see Ollie again soon. I wonder if I should text him? He probably doesn't want to chat with me right now. I hope he comes back soon. But what difference will that even make?

CHAPTER 27

I come up with a plan. The plan is that I'll run every day between now and the race, just adding one minute at a time. And I carry out the plan. It becomes my single-minded mission. I don't even have Ollie to help me stay motivated, but I've decided that I don't need him. I mean, I would *like* him to be here, but this challenge was never about him—it was about me. So I focus and I push myself, and every day I get a little bit better.

And then suddenly the race is two days away.

"You sure you don't want to do it?" I ever so casually ask Liv one more time while we're hanging out at mine.

"I'm sure! Anyway, it's too late for me to register."

At least I registered on time. "Huh, that reminds me," I say, getting up and retrieving Mum's laptop from the coffee table.

"What?" Liv asks. She's sprawled out on one sofa while I resettle myself on the other, open the laptop, and try to remember the bloody URL for our school email login.

"I left my registration to Ollie and I wasn't sure if he actually did it, so I sent an email a couple of days ago to check that they got it," I say, furrowing my brow. I'm sure it doesn't matter. It's not like I *need* a reply, but still.

Sasha pads in. “Hey, squirt,” I say to her, looking up from the laptop. “Sasha, this is my friend Liv. Liv, this is my cool little sister, Sasha.”

“Hi, Sasha,” says Liv. “You *are* cool. I like your shorts.” Liv nods at her sequined gold shorts. There isn’t a hint of condescension in Liv’s voice. She actually sounds like she *does* think Sasha looks cool.

“Thanks,” Sasha says, beaming. “What are you watching?” She slides into the armchair, at which point we pause *Uncut Gems* on the grounds it is not suitable for her ten-year-old eyes.

“Nothing,” I say with a yawn. “I’m tired.”

Sasha huffs in the way only a ten-year-old can. “Of *course* you’re tired! You need to take a break from running!”

I laugh. “I guess you’re right, Squirtle.”

“You’re definitely right,” Liv says, high-fiving her.

I’m actually glad about someone telling me what to do, even if it is Sasha. I need that direction in my life, and since Ollie went away, I haven’t really had that. Maybe it wasn’t so smart to push myself like this, but, whatever, I need all the help I can get to face the race on Sunday.

I finally make it into my email inbox and . . . “Shit!” I say louder than I mean to. “That absolute shithead!”

“What?” Liv asks, looking concerned.

I stare at the screen in disbelief. “Mr. bloody Pearce replied to my email saying that he assumed that Ollie had registered me as a joke! What a . . .” I want to go for something stronger than my usual, but with Sasha in the room, I must resist.

“Sorry, but that’s just nonsense,” Liv says, looking furious on my behalf. “Why would he send you that? What does he even get out of this? It’s like he doesn’t *want* people to get involved.”

“Ollie signed me up because I wasn’t sure if I could get into my school emails! He did it to help me! But Mr. Pearce just assumed it was some elaborate form of cyberbullying," I say, exasperated. "He's never even met Ollie! He hasn't even started at Dawson yet! Why would he be cyberbullying me?!"

"What's happening? I'm confused," Sasha says with a pained expression.

"Yeah, what's the beef?" Jake emerges at the most annoying possible moment. I suppose it's his right, since he lives here, but I would rather he just stayed in his cave.

"One of the horrible PE teachers from our school is trying to put me off running the race this weekend. The one I've been training for."

"Why would a *teacher* do that?" Sasha asks.

"He thinks someone put me forward as a joke, which is stupid," I say. "Well, I guess I'll just have to reply and say, *No, it is not a joke. I am dead serious and I will see you on Sunday to kick your butt.*"

Sasha laughs. Liv just glares at the TV. Jake shrugs and slopes off into the kitchen.

As I write my reply—minus the butt-kicking part—I'm filled with righteous indignation but also . . . a nagging doubt. What if he's right? What if I can't actually do this on Sunday? Five kilometers sounds like a really long way, and I haven't been tracking my runs so I don't even know if I've *run* five kilometers. All of this is suddenly feeling very real. I'm in this situation and I can't get out of it now, but also I don't want to get out of it, but also why am I even doing this in the first place, but also the Jakes and the Mr. Pearces of the world need to be taken down a peg or two, but also I have to actually be *able* to take them down a peg or two, but also but also but also . . .

I feel like I'm being crushed under the sheer weight of how other people perceive me. I know who I am and I know what I can do if I set my mind to it, but it just feels like at every turn there's someone who wants to remind me how bad and wrong and defective I am because of the body that I have. It's too much sometimes. It's too much today.

I hear keys in the lock. "Hello, babies!" Mum calls, lugging in shopping bags with about twenty blocks of butter.

"Hi, Mum," I say. "My friend Liv is here. Hope that's OK."

"That's fine with me. Are you staying for dinner, Liv?"

Liv shifts from her comfy slouch to a more formal seated position. "Oh, no, thank you. It's my mum's birthday so we're going out for dinner. But thanks so much for asking me," she says extremely politely. Mum will like that.

"Oooh, lovely! Where are you going?" she asks, absent-mindedly stroking Sasha's hair.

"Well, we always used to go to the Italian place in Crystal Palace on her birthday, but since that closed down we've been going to a place in Brockley, which isn't as nice, but where is?" she says, shrugging.

"Ha!" I say. "You know that was Ollie's parents' place?"

"The Ollie that you fancy and also go running with?" Liv asks, which makes me blush furiously.

"Yes," I mumble, "that one."

"Ooooh, Ruby's got a *boyfriend*." Sasha giggles, so I flick at her with my foot.

"No, I don't. I really, definitely don't."

"He'll be back any day now," says Mum sagely. "He texted me to say he would be home in time to do next week's deliveries, but you have school on Monday, so I told him I only want him to keep it up if it doesn't interfere with his schoolwork."

My head feels hot and hazy. Of course Ollie has to come back any day now, since school is starting again after the weekend.

"But he'll still be doing deliveries?" I ask.

"Yes, why not?" Mum frowns at me. I guess she never got dragged into the whole has-Ollie-been-crushed-by-the-wheels-of-a-bus situation the other week.

"No reason," I say, and no one says anything for a moment.

"Anyway," Liv says, lifting herself up, "I should get going."

"Do you need a ride?" Mum asks. Now, most parents would not mean it when they ask this question, but Mum *loves* driving. She would have been doing her local deliveries herself if she had the time.

"No, it's OK," Liv says. "I like the walk. It was nice to meet you." She turns to Sasha. "And you." And on her way out she puts her hands on my shoulders. "See *you* on Sunday. Don't panic. And no more running. Oh, and is April gonna be there?"

I smile, feeling present in the moment again at last rather than swirling around inside my own head. "Yeah, she'll be there. I'm sure I can put you in the same place at the same time in a way that wouldn't be completely mortifying."

"I've never been mortified in my life," Liv says, and I almost believe her.

After dinner I dash upstairs to retrieve my phone so I can half watch TV with Mum and half waste time scrolling. Sasha's door is slightly ajar, and I swear I'm not being nosy, but I catch sight of her reflection in the mirror as I pass. She's standing sideways, looking at herself, sucking in her tummy and standing on tiptoes. I wonder what's going on inside her head, what fantasies of some future self are brewing in there. I put my hand on the door, trying to decide if I should make my presence known. But I don't know what to say. I don't know how to keep her afloat when it's an everyday effort for me too. I suppose I'll just have to lead by example, won't I?

CHAPTER 28

I do as Liv and Sasha told me. I don't go running, but I do go skating with April and Jessica and Salma. There is *much* excitement and giggling about the prospect of April and Liv meeting.

"It's really happening!" Jess squeals.

"So she'll definitely be there tomorrow?" April asks as we whizz around the flat concrete part of the skate park. This is not the first time she's asked.

"She says she will," I tell her.

"I can't believe she was there the whole time and you liked her and you never even bothered to talk to her," Salma says, sipping on a blue slushy from the ice cream van. Always blue.

"Love works in mysterious ways," April says, shrugging then regretting the shrug as it makes her wobble a bit, but she rights herself rather than falling over.

"I miss the days when I was, like, even vaguely hopeful . . ." I say wistfully.

"You mean, like, two weeks ago?" Jessica prompts. She's doing some skating that involves crossing and uncrossing her legs in front of her as she moves. It looks extremely cool.

"Yeah, exactly. The good old days."

"You know what would make me absolutely scream with horror?" Jess says. "If you fell today and broke your ankle and couldn't run after you've spent all summer training for the Dash."

"Oh my days!" says Salma. "Don't even joke about that!"

"I literally thought the exact same thing this morning when I was getting ready to come out," I say, laughing. "And I was like . . . well, that would be a good excuse not to do it, but then I realized that I really *want* to do it now. Like, I've put all this effort in and I feel like I actually really *enjoy* running."

"Have you lost any weight?" Salma asks, taking another sip.

I feel like someone's just skated right into me and knocked me to the ground. "No?" I frown at her. "I mean, I don't know? I wasn't, like, trying to? I mean, it wasn't part of the plan."

She shrugs. "Oh, OK. I guess I just thought it was." Jessica has skated out of earshot, but April is looking at me like *What the hell?*

"No . . . not really. I mean, not at all."

"OK," she says again. And I realize that for her, this was just a pretty neutral topic of conversation, but for me it has . . . well, it has a lot of *weight* to it. It makes me feel even more grateful to have Liv in my life.

Although the conversation moves on, and we skate together for another half an hour or so, my brain feels elsewhere.

April and I walk toward home together, and as we're walking down Sydenham Avenue, I think of when I saw Liv walking the dog on the other side of the street earlier in the summer. It makes me realize how far I've come since then.

"That was weird, right?" April says.

"Salma?" I ask.

"Yeah. Or was it not? Sorry if I'm, like, projecting or whatever."

"No, it was a bit weird. It just made me understand that even people who care about me don't always fully get it, right? Does that make sense?"

"Yeah, it makes sense."

"You know who's really cool about this stuff?"

"Is it Liv?" she says, grinning.

"It is. Ugh, I miss having a crush on Ollie!"

"What happened to the crush?" she asks.

"I don't know . . . I mean, nothing, really, like the crush is still *there*. It just feels so useless now. Like, I haven't seen him in a couple of weeks and I still really like him, but it's just . . . not gonna happen, is it? Not that it ever was."

"You have to stop talking about my best friend like that," she says. "You're a cool badass babe and he would be lucky to go out with you. I swear."

"Thanks, dude," I say, trying to believe her.

We part ways, April saying she'll see me tomorrow at the race, and when I get home, I realize with a jolt that Ollie's family car is parked outside the house. Of course it is. We're back at school in two days' time. But I just hadn't thought about the fact that his coming home was literally inevitable. He's just in there, right now. Just sitting there. I guess I'll see him at the Dash tomorrow. God, I'm really doing it. TO! MOR! ROW! I feel my stomach lurch with the understanding that it's really happening. I can't back out now, not after I've been talking such a big game about it for weeks. What was I thinking telling my brother I could *win* the race? No, come on. It's Liv I need to channel at a time like this, not Jake.

For the rest of the evening, I'm going to think positively. By this time tomorrow, it'll all be over, so if I'm going through with it, I have to start thinking like a winner or something. Maybe I should watch some motivational videos, some bodybuilder or cult leader telling me that *I can do it!*

"Hey, Freckle Face," Jake says as I close the door behind me.

"Hey." I shrug my bag with my skates onto the floor. "How come you're not at the pub?"

"I got the sack," he says, not taking his eyes off the TV. "Just kidding, they wouldn't dare. I'm off tonight. Going for drinks with the boys later, though."

"Fun," I say with a hint of skepticism, and am glad I won't be in whatever pub Jake and his friends end up in. "Where's Mum?"

"She's out. Dropping Sasha at some birthday party. I'm making us dinner before I go and leaving some for Mum when she gets back from picking up Sasha."

"Cool, let me know if you need any help," I say, already disappearing upstairs.

"From you?" Jake calls back. "No way."

At dinnertime, I slink downstairs to set the table. "That smells good," I tell him, because it does, and I'm not *so* petty that I can't give my annoying brother a compliment.

"I got mad skills," he says, yanking on an oven glove to pull a lasagna out of the oven.

I put some salad in a bowl. "Just me and you, yeah?"

"Yep," he says, slicing into it.

"Looks good too," I say as I start laying out our knives and forks on the dining table. See? We *are* capable of playing nice!

Jake emerges from the kitchen and sets down our plates.

I sigh. "Is this a joke?" I ask, rolling my eyes.

"No, why?" he asks nonchalantly.

I look down at my plate. Then back up at him. "Really?" I say.

The quantity of food on my plate can barely be seen by the naked eye. Well, OK, I exaggerate, but you know what I mean. A tiny square, like a bloody millionaire's shortbread.

Jake sighs. "You can get more if you want," he says with a shrug. "I just thought that you were taking this *whole thing* seriously."

I know in an instant what he's trying to say. He's hoping that my doing the Dawson Dash is a full personality transplant, my pathway into being the kind of person he can respect, rather than just something I'm doing. I feel my blood pressure rising. "What you think of as a *whole thing* is something I try not to worry about at all. I try really, really hard actually!"

"Maybe you need to stop trying," he says, putting down his knife and fork and folding his arms over his chest.

We stare at each other for a moment across a huge divide. I want to make myself understood, but I know that I just can't. It's too much for him. It's too much for a lot of people. I know that. But why is it so hard to just let me do my thing?

"You can't get your head around it, can you? The idea that I'm not miserable in a body like this!" Jake just looks at me skeptically. "Yes, maybe *you* were! But I'm not!"

He shakes his head. "I just don't believe you," he says, smirking. "I think you're lying to yourself."

"And I can't prove that I'm not, so that means you can just go on believing it, projecting all your bullshit onto me."

"It's not just about you, though, is it? It's Sasha as well!"

"Exactly! You're affecting Sasha as well! Thank God she isn't here right now because she doesn't need to hear this from anyone, let alone in her own home!"

"No, I mean, you're *brainwashing* her! You know it's unhealthy, right? All of this . . . 'positivity' of yours?" He puts mocking air quotes around *positivity* because of course he does.

"You think making a child paranoid about their weight is healthy?"

"It's not about making her paranoid," he says, rolling his eyes like I'm so obviously very stupid indeed. "I just don't want her growing up and swallowing all your nonsense and regretting it."

"Why would she regret it? This makes no sense!"

"Look, it's not that hard. You could lose weight if you wanted to. I did," he says, shrugging. "I'm loads happier now."

"Is that maybe because people are nicer to you because you're not fat? And would the solution *perhaps* be to treat people like people regardless of what their body looks like?" I spit out the words at him.

A cloud passes over his face. "No . . ." he says, frowning. "I mean, if it's not that hard, why don't you just *try* it?"

"Because I don't want to!" I shout. "Isn't it enough that I'm jumping through these ridiculous hoops for you? To prove to you that I don't *need* to lose weight to do all this shit? Isn't that enough? Any normal person would see that it's *too much*! But, no, you have to pile all this extra shit on top of me! I don't know when it'll end! I don't know how much more I have to do to prove to you that you should respect me because I'm a person! That you should care about Sasha's mind and happiness because she's your sister and you love her! That all this stuff about weight that's clearly been tormenting you your whole life is just . . . made up! You don't have to play the game!"

He stares at me, his nostrils flaring. "You just sound crazy," he says, shaking his head. "Go on, get more food, eat the whole thing. I don't care—I know you want to."

"I don't *want* to! I just want you to treat me like a person, not a failed experiment! If you keep treating everyone like this, then no one will care about you and you'll deserve it!" I yell, pushing my chair back and standing up in a white-hot rage. I start walking toward the stairs.

"Yeah, maybe," says Jake. I turn to look at him over my shoulder, not wanting to give him the attention of turning my whole body around. "But at least I'm not fat."

And with that I give up. I thought I was getting through to him. I thought even if not for my sake then maybe he could see it differently for Sasha's. I take refuge in my room and I don't come out for the rest of the evening. Even though Jake's gone out, I just stay in my room, getting more and more worked up. Not to mention hungrier and hungrier. I don't even stir from my nest when Mum and Sasha come home. I watch episodes of TV shows I've seen hundreds of times before in the hope they'll reset my angry brain, but nothing works. I pick up my phone to message Liv but don't really know what I want from her. Well, I guess I want comfort and reassurance, but I can't just run to her every time someone's a shit to me.

Eventually I've stewed long enough that it's time for bed. But I'm not tired. I need to sleep, though, don't I?

I lie perfectly still, trying to drift off to sleep. But my mind is full and it's racing and I can't make it stop. I want to sneak downstairs and get myself something to eat, but I don't want to chance bumping into anyone, so I just stay here. I toss and turn before remembering I was trying to lie perfectly still, and I try to evacuate my brain of all thoughts, but that's hard! I can't do it! I'm too full of them fizzing around in my head. Can I get out of the race tomorrow? Of course I can . . . it's a free country . . . But it would be embarrassing. It would prove Jake right. And that's the last thing I want to do after this evening. I just need to sleep. I barely feel ready to run the race as it is, let alone without resting.

Everything feels so heavy. The weight of trying to make things better for Sasha. Trying to fend off all the harmful messages directed at me and my body. Maybe it's too much. Maybe I can't do it. Maybe I can't carry it all anymore. Maybe I can't keep Sasha feeling strong. Maybe I don't have it in me. I can't do it. I'm not cut out for this. Who was I even kidding?

CHAPTER 29

I'm running the race. It's the Dawson Dash and I'm running, I'm running, I'm running . . . I'm in the lead! Way out in front! But I'm not wearing any shoes! Why am I not wearing shoes? It's hard to run when you're not wearing shoes. Everyone else has their trainers on. And someone's shouting my name. But . . . not really shouting. *Ruby! Ruby?* It sounds close, right near my ear . . . But everyone's behind the ribbons . . .

"Ruby?" The voice from my dream. "Roo?" A gentle voice but insistent. A voice I know well. My mum's voice. My eyes snap open.

"What?" I say, jumping out of my skin at the sight of Mum bent over the bed. "Who's dead?"

"No one's dead, but . . . isn't it your race today?"

"Yeah . . ." I mumble. "But I don't want to go. I don't have to, do I?"

She frowns. "No. I wouldn't ever make you if you didn't want to."

I swallow hard. "OK." I nod. "I don't want to."

She steps back from the bed and folds her arms across her chest. "Are you sure?"

But before I can answer, Sasha comes barreling into my room. "HURRY UP, RUBY! It's your race today!"

And there's just something about the expectant look on her

face, the wide, urging eyes. She's at least half the reason I've put myself through all this! I can't flake now.

"Come on!" she says, yanking my duvet off me. "You'll be late!"

"Why, what time is it?"

Mum grimaces. "Ten fifteen."

"Shit! It starts at eleven! Can you drive me? I was going to walk, but . . . shit!" I jump out of bed, literally *jump*. I start rummaging around for some socks . . . Gotta have socks . . . Where are my leggings?

"Of course I'll drive you! Why were you even going to walk when I'll be driving there anyway?"

"Why? You're not coming to watch it, are you?"

"Of course I am!" she says. "We all are!"

"Yeah!" Sasha says enthusiastically before bouncing out of the room again.

"Even Jake?" I say, remembering the cause of my bad night's sleep.

"Well, yes!"

"Ugggggh," I say. I barely want to get out of bed, let alone Do the Thing, especially not in front of Jake, who seems to have no interest in abandoning his goal of humiliating me.

"Will you be ready to go in ten minutes?"

"I guess I'll have to be," I say. The adrenaline of being suddenly woken from my sleep has barely worn off. I'm sure I can get all my stuff together in ten minutes.

"That'll give us half an hour to get there," Mum says.

"That's fine, right? It's only in Dulwich."

"Just get a move on!" Mum says, standing in the doorway, her hands on her hips. "I'll make sure Jake and Sasha are ready to go."

I scramble around my room, finding my sports bra, my lucky

underwear, my leggings, my trainers, a T-shirt. I get dressed in record time and run downstairs, where Jake is sitting on the sofa on his phone and Sasha's filling my water bottle for me.

"Come on!" Mum says, holding the front door open so we can all pile out and into the car, but I notice something on the table next to the door that's piled with various things we might need upon leaving the house. A shiny red box wrapped with a ribbon.

"What's that?" I ask.

"I don't know. I didn't open it," Mum says. "The label says *Ruby*."

"Oh." I frown, wondering if I have time to see what's inside.

"Quick! If you're going to open it now, do it quickly."

I do as she says and yank off the ribbon and open the box to find a pile of cookies dusted in fine powdered sugar. And a note in tidy handwriting.

Hi, Ruby,

This is just to say how much I missed you while I was away. I didn't know my nonno (or grandad, if you don't know what that means!) very well, but when I was in Italy my mum found all these recipe cards he had written for the things he loved to make so he wouldn't forget how. These are my version of his ricciarelli, and I think I did them justice (with some help from my mum, who I think understands me a bit better now). Anyway, I really, really hope you're still going to run the Dash, and I'm sorry I wasn't there for you when it was important.

Ollie

• • • • •

I feel completely lightheaded, like all the blood in my body has rushed to my face.

"Well, come on!" Mum urges me, and I set the box down on the table.

"What was it?" she asks over her shoulder as she locks up.

"It was from Ollie . . ." I say in disbelief.

"Well, well, well," she says with a smile.

Even in our haste to get on the road, I notice the Cowan family car isn't there, so I guess Ollie is on his way, if not *there* by now. Shit! How did this happen?!

Once we get going after a brief argument about who's going to sit in the front seat (always Jake or me, never Sasha, naturally), I start to feel *properly* nervous. It's the not-being-able-to-do-anything part of the day. I know I could flake out at any moment, just decide I don't want to go through with it. But I'm committed. I watch Dartmouth Road zoom by until we get to the traffic lights outside Forest Hill Station. We wait. And we wait. And we wait. The race starts in twenty minutes. I feel myself sweating. *Come on, come on,* I think. Which makes me really understand that I do want to get there in time. I do want to take part. And finally the lights change! We crawl past the big pub to the set of traffic lights outside Sainsbury's, where Ollie's mum thought he had been knocked over. And then there's another set of traffic lights before the Horniman. It's just one after another—how are we ever going to get off this cursed stretch of road?! But we do get off it, and then it's plain sailing around to St. Alfred's, where the car park is heaving, nearly full. But we get a space, and as I dash out of the back seat (obviously I lost the skirmish with Jake for the front seat), I call to Mum that I'll see her afterward.

I notice that a route has been marked out with cones and flags in the main field. I'm nearly at the registration table when Liv ambles into view. I equally don't have time to chat and desperately need to chat. About my nerves, about my fight with Jake, about Ollie, about everything.

"Oh my God, I thought you weren't coming!" Liv says, throwing her arms around me. She's wearing another cool athleisure look. Maybe while I was oversleeping, she's been running in Dulwich Park like we did the other week. I wish that was my morning's activity. No competition required. I'm about to tell her how cool she looks when she asks, "How are you feeling? Peppy? Zingy? On top of the world, ready to dominate?"

"Ummm . . ." I say. "Not really. This morning has been a mess. I had a weird horrible fight with my brother last night and nearly overslept this morning and then something strange happened just before I left the house, which is, like, *good,* but I don't really know how good. My head is just not in the game."

"So you need me to get in your brain, right? OK, got it. You are a beautiful, powerful angel and you've worked hard to get to this very moment and now is your time to capitalize on all your hard work and let your body do its thing."

I look around nervously at all the actual sporty girls in their sports bras and Lycra shorts and I feel completely ridiculous. These are girls who play football or are on the tennis team or run for the county. It's just not me. I don't know why I ever thought I could do this.

"Now that I'm here . . ." I say, not looking her in the eye, "I just feel kind of stupid."

"Why?" she says, putting her hands on her hips. "Because you don't look like everyone else who's running today? Who cares!

You don't care! You only care when you compare yourself to other people, which is the quickest way to"—she makes a slurping noise like a Hoover swallowing a puddle—"suck up all the joy from your life. You deserve to be here as much as anyone else. You deserve to take part. If you believe you don't, that's because people like Mr. Pearce have brainwashed you. You've enjoyed getting here, right?"

"Yes," I mumble, because it's true. I *have* enjoyed it. She's right. She is, to be fair, always right.

"So that's it. That's all there is to it. You have as much right to be here as they do. This is *for you* as much as it is for anyone else. This is your life, and you've got to do this shit on your own terms. Yeah?"

"Yeah," I say, and I realize I'm smiling. I can't help it.

"OK, then," she says, giving me a decisive nod. "I'm going to walk over to some bit of the track where you might be grateful to see my fat face."

"I'm always grateful to see your fat face," I say, and I mean it with every fiber of my being. "Oh, and look out for April, she'll be here somewhere."

"Nuh-uh," she says, shaking her head. "First we deal with you, then we deal with me."

She stomps off to find a good watching point just as Jessica bounds up to me.

"There you are!" She throws her arms around my shoulders. "Are you excited?"

"That's one word for it . . ." I say with a grimace.

"You've trained so hard! It's going to be fine, I promise."

"I know." I nod, even though I don't know that it's going to be fine.

"Don't forget you have to go to the table! I've already done my registration, so I'll see you at the starting line! You know, we're all really proud of you already."

"Got it," I tell her, and take a deep breath before striding over to register.

"Well, well, well," says Mr. Pearce from behind the table.

"Hello, sir," I say quickly. "I'm not too late, am I?"

He sighs wearily. "No, Ruby, you're not too late. I'm just surprised you turned up at all," he says, ticking my name off the list. "You're not planning some sort of . . . political protest, are you?"

It's like he literally can't comprehend the idea that I might want to take part! Maybe he believes so much in his own ability to put people like me off any kind of physical activity that he can't get his brain around it. It's taken a lot for me to get my brain around it too, but there is a big part of me that just wants to prove him wrong today.

When I've finished registration, I catch sight of Mum and Jake and Sasha making their way onto the field. Mum waves at me and they come over.

"You were in such a hurry that I thought I wasn't even going to be able to wish you luck!" Mum says.

"Good luck, Roo," says Sasha, throwing her arms around me and leaning her head against my chest like she used to when she was really little. "I think you can win," she whispers into my flesh.

"Thanks, Sash," I whisper back. I admire her optimism.

I look to Jake, expecting to see a hard smirk, some arrogant pose. But he just nods at me and says, "Good luck." It even sounds like he means it.

I check my phone before entrusting it to Mum to look after while I run. There's a text. My heart jumps when I see it's from Ollie.

Where are you? Please don't tell me you've given up. You can do this. Just get here.

I don't reply. I don't have time. But shielding my eyes from the bright sunshine, I scan the assembled bodies at the starting line for his familiar lanky ginger presence. There are just too many people around. I can't see him at all. I know he must be here somewhere. And I know he wants to see me.

"Runners!" comes Mr. Pearce's voice over a loudspeaker. I can see him flanked by some of his other PE teacher minions, like Miss Flowers, Mr. Boateng, and Mrs. Zimmer, who are all standing around looking mean in sweatpants. Sweatpants? In this weather? Treat yourself to some shorts, I beg you. "Please make your way over to the starting line. The route has been marked out for you. It is precisely one-third of the total five-kilometer distance. You must complete three full laps in order to finish. The first three runners over the finish line will be awarded their prizes once everyone has completed the course."

As I make my way over to the start, I try to stay calm and not convince myself that everyone is looking at me, wondering why I'm there, wondering if Mr. Pearce is right and it's some joke or form of protest. I mean . . . it *is* a protest in a way. But I'm here because I can be. I'm here because I'm allowed to be. It's a space for me too. Like Liv said, it's as much for me as it is for anyone. I take deep breaths and congregate around the starting line with everyone else. It feels like there are hundreds of people here, but there are probably, I don't know, maybe fifty? I am not faster than fifty people in my year. Why am I here, why am I here, why am I here?

"Three," says Mr. Pearce through the loudspeaker when he sees we're all assembled. My heart rate jumps with nerves.

"Two."

Oh God, I'm really doing this, aren't I?

"One!"

CHAPTER 30

I set off. We're all moving. I'm moving. I'm picking up my feet and running. But not too fast. Just steady. The group seems to be moving as one, staying in a herd formation. I look over my shoulder as I move away from the starting line, which is also the finish line. That's where most people seem to be clustering, but my family members are moving away from the crowd and positioning themselves just past the halfway marker.

I turn my head back to my direction of travel, and I'm pretty sure I can see Jessica over to my left. Of course she's going to smash it today. But where's Ollie? I know he must be here somewhere. I'm grateful for the distraction of trying to find him because it wastes a few minutes of running time. *Where's Wally?* is out. *Where's Ollie?* is in. Is that him? I think I spot him right at the front of the pack. I didn't realize he was quite *that* fast. It's definitely him. It's strange to see him among so many people, when for so long it was always just me and him. Just his attention and care trained on me. And for what? What did he ever get out of it? Nothing. God, I hope I can fix things with him. I missed him while he was away, and now I'll have no excuse to hang out with him at all, if he even wants to. I swirl around in my head for a few minutes, just putting one foot in front of the other while my brain thinks about Ollie, and when I snap back into the moment, I realize . . . I'm almost alone.

Everyone is so far ahead of me.

They've all just peeled away and gone at their own pace, which is so much faster than mine because of course it is, because this is a *race,* because they're made for this and I'm not. It only took maybe five minutes for this to become apparent. I can see the halfway mark ahead of me. That means I'm not even halfway through the first lap. Shit.

The course is an oval, with the halfway mark on the opposite side from the starting and finish line, and on the other side of the halfway mark I can see the other runners, the fast ones, the good ones, just steadily pushing on, looking like it comes completely naturally to them. Jess's braids are swinging as she runs—she's laser-focused on the task ahead. Not a wandering lazy brain like me. And there he is, Ollie, somewhere near the front. Maybe not in actual first place but not far off. That's how fast he should have been going this whole time. That's his speed. And I'm doing mine. We're too different, aren't we?

I see him turn his head to the side to wipe his forehead on the sleeve of his T-shirt. That's when he catches a glimpse of me plodding at my very Ruby pace right at the back. Embarrassingly at the back. I feel mortified at being seen by him and can only bear to look at him like that for a second before taking a deep breath and pressing forward. I'm not *so* far behind everyone. I just need to push on.

Just before I reach the halfway mark, I see Mr. Boateng is standing next to a bright pink flag. Beyond him I think I can see the top of Liv's bouncy blond halo of curls. I realize she's standing next to April and Salma. Well, at least *someone* is having a good time right now. All this effort will have been worth it if those two hit it off!

I know my family members are congregated somewhere between the halfway marker and the start/finish, and the thought of having to make eye contact with any of them at this particular moment is what keeps my gaze fixed on the path ahead. I hear cheers of encouragement, but I can't look. I can't see their expressions. I just have to keep going.

I haven't made it far past the starting line for the second of my three laps when I hear a roar of applause behind me. At least one person has already finished. And I still have just under two-thirds to go. Wow. I really am on a different planet. But at least right now I'm briefly amid the pack of runners—the people who are now on their third lap while I'm on my second. I have to savor this moment of blending into the crowd because I know in no time at all they're going to all pull ahead while I am incapable of doing so, and I'll be alone again.

By the halfway marker I'm proven right. I'm plodding along on my own while they're all way, way ahead of me, hitting the finish line. I'm just over halfway through the race, but the thought doesn't fortify me—it makes me want to lie down and cry at the effort I've already expended and all the emotions I've already felt with so much distance left to go. I get my head down and keep going toward the starting line and my third and final lap.

When I cross it, I can't help but wonder how many people are still running. There must be a few people ahead of me on this lap. I can't be the only person still going. Maybe I am. Maybe I am just that much slower than everyone else. Which begs the questions: Can I really do this *another* time? Can I bear to put myself through this while I'm so far behind everyone else—when almost everyone else has already finished? Not just the good people, like Ollie and Jess, who very obviously have already finished, but everyone. I am alone. Properly alone.

I feel a hot wave of humiliation wash over me. This feels exactly like the sprints in that worst-ever PE lesson, and I don't know why I thought it would feel any different. I was always going to be the slowest one, the odd one out, the one who just couldn't keep up. Tears prick at my eyes. There's a lump in my throat.

This isn't like running around the park with Ollie, going at my own pace. This is something completely new. The eyes of all these people are on me. The knowledge that I'm here of my own choice. But the thing is, it's not like I *physically* want to give up yet. It's just . . . emotionally.

I could duck out now, couldn't I? No one would even be surprised if I just ground to a halt. Just stopped running. Just gave up. It would be exactly what they were expecting, in fact. Especially Jake, and he's pretty much the reason why I'm here. I could just stop and cross the line of cones and flags, and join April and Salma in the crowd. I could go to my family and hold my hands up and say, "Well, you were right!" I could do that. Just cross the line into the spectators.

But then the opposite happens. From behind the line of cones, I see someone jog from the spectator side into the runners' side.

Liv.

"You're not on your own anymore," she says. "We can do this together. But you're *not* allowed to give up."

She pulls off her T-shirt and tosses it over her shoulder to April, who catches it.

"Go on, Ruby!" April shouts at me.

"Yeah!" Salma yells, clapping. "Go on, Roo!"

"You've got this!" April jumps up and down in a very un-April way.

Liv and I run side by side. Slowly. But we keep going. I offer her my water bottle, and she takes a sip before handing it back to me. We stay focused on the track ahead. We don't speak for a while. We just run. Together.

"This was . . . one way . . . to impress April," I say to Liv through ragged breathing.

"Oh yeah . . . It was my plan . . . all along," she says.

When I hear Sasha shout, "It's Ruby!" I can't help but smile. I realize we're nearly done. We're nearly at the finish line.

"Come on, Roo!" Mum calls out to me.

And to my great surprise, Jake cups his hands around his mouth and shouts, "You're doing great! You can do this!"

But there's an even greater surprise. A voice I know well but don't hear so often anymore. Could it really be my dad? I can't look. I just have to get over the finish line.

My lungs feel like they're going to give up. Every muscle in my legs is begging me to stop. But I don't. I don't care how slowly I have to finish this. I am going to finish it. I can finish this. I just put my head down and keep going. All I have to do is not stop. That's it. Just don't stop. The only thing I have to do is not stop. I'm not going to stop. I'm not going to stop. And then, out of nowhere, the finish line goes from the horizon to right in front of us. Only a few more steps. I can hardly believe it.

I grab Liv's hand in my sweaty palm and we run the last few steps together and all our people are cheering and clapping and finally, finally my foot passes the finish line for the last time.

I did it. I won.

I don't need a medal, or a £100 prize, or to prove my brother wrong, or to steal his bedroom off him in a bet. I just needed to show myself that rules and limits imposed by other people are not for me. They're for them. I can find joy and pain and highs and lows and good days and bad days just the way I am. I get to decide what I can and can't do.

And today I decide that I win.

CHAPTER 31

For a second we just stand there panting and grinning at each other. Liv drops my hand and doubles over, trying to get her breath back. I can barely believe I did it. Ruby Morgan running the Dawson Dash? Who would ever have thought it? Well, I guess a few people did. Ollie and Liv for starters. And in that moment, I am so full of love and pride and happiness that I feel like I could float away. I want to ride this wave.

As if I'm not euphoric enough, I see Ollie jogging toward me, looking decidedly less sweaty than me but no less happy. Sweatier and redder than I've ever been in my life, I take Ollie's hand and pull him toward me. I kiss him gently on the lips. If he wants to pull away, then he can. I'm not going to stop him. I'm not going to be surprised.

But he doesn't. He kisses me back. He wraps his arms around me and kisses me insistently, like he really means it. I can hear my friends whoop and cheer like we're still running the race.

"This isn't . . . really what I thought it would be like," he says, smiling, as we separate.

"The race?" I ask, my heart pounding.

"No, our first kiss," he says, rolling his eyes like it's completely obvious.

"I didn't know you had thought about it at all."

He shrugs. "I thought the heart-shaped cookies might be a bit of a giveaway. But I figured it was worth a try . . . even though for a while there I thought you were more interested in Liv, you know, in that way . . ."

"Nah, she's just extremely cool. I'm leaving the romance side of things to April."

I don't want to take my eyes off him, but there's so much going on around me.

Liv! I grasp Liv to me in the tightest hug I've ever managed. "Thank you, thank you, thank you." We pull apart.

She looks at me and swallows, embarrassed by the attention. "It's nothing. Anytime. I'm Liv," she says, turning to Ollie. "Nice to meet you."

"You too. That was . . . very cool of you," he says, a little in awe of her. I know how he feels. But I know Liv wouldn't want me to feel like that. To her we're the same, even if to me she's this beautiful perfect inspirational angel.

I still haven't figured out what to say to Ollie when we're interrupted. Suddenly everyone is on top of us. April and Salma and Sasha and Mum and Jake and . . . yes, Dad. Ollie can wait.

The group is a whirlwind of chatter and hugs and animation, and I'm not sure which way I'm meant to be looking or who I'm meant to be talking to. Then Sasha's chubby hand finds mine.

"Sorry I didn't win, matey," I say to her, frowning.

She rolls her eyes at me like she's really grown-up. "Winning is *not even important*, you know. But you looked really cool. And you did something Jake said you couldn't do, but I knew you could."

"Jake thinks I did it to impress him, but I think I mostly did it to impress you," I say.

She nods resolutely. "I'm impressed. Is he your boyfriend?" she asks, turning to look at Ollie, who's chatting to his parents nearby.

It's my turn to shrug nonchalantly. "I'm not sure yet. But I hope so. It's OK if he's not, though."

"I hope so too. *Anyway*," she says with a weary sigh, and once again I'm forced to wonder where she learns to do this, "I want to go see Dad. Bye." And with that, she stalks off.

I want to see Dad too! But now I can see Jake in lively conversation with Mr. Pearce, who doesn't look quite as pleased to see his star pupil as I thought he would. I'm trying to make out what they're saying when Salma and Jessica bound over to me with all the energy of two Labrador puppies. Salma I can understand, but how does Jessica have that much left in her after the race?!

I hug Jess, the bronze medal around her neck swaying against my body. "You did amazing! Well done, mate," I say.

She beams. "Thank you, thank you, thank you! I feel amazing. I didn't think I was actually going to come in third!" Over her shoulder I notice April and Liv in conversation, April still holding Liv's T-shirt that she caught during the race. Everything is happening all at once! "Anyway, listen to this!" Jess turns to Salma, who looks like she's about to explode with the need to tell me whatever she's about to tell me.

"Oh my *days*!" Salma begins at last. "I just overheard your fit brother getting into beef with Mr. Pearce!" I look over and Jake is stalking away from him, shaking his head.

"What?" I say, frowning.

"She heard it!" Jessica says emphatically.

"I heard it!" Salma echoes.

"Tell me!" I say, even though I'm too deliriously happy from the race and the kiss and EVERYTHING to be too interested in what Jake is up to.

"Mr. Pearce was saying to him that, uh"—she averts her eyes for a moment—"that you ran the slowest time in the history of the Dawson Dash. By a long way."

"Ha!" I say. Of course I did. I'm not embarrassed!

"And it was like he was trying to get Jake to join in and laugh at you . . . and instead Jake was just like, Well, maybe if you tried harder to include everyone, then maybe it wouldn't just be the really sporty lot who want to get involved. That maybe now more people would get involved because they want to, even if they're not, like, Dawson-athlete types."

"Oh," I say, frowning.

"And Mr. Pearce was like, Well that's the last thing we want, more jokers not taking it seriously. And *Jake* was like, My sister is not a joker. She's the bravest and most dedicated person here! And Mr. Pearce went *bright* red and just kept opening and closing his mouth like a fish! And then I ran over to tell you about it. So that's it. But that's sick, right?!"

"Very unexpected," I murmur.

Maybe she didn't hear him right. Maybe she misunderstood. But when Jake emerges by my side a moment later, I know Salma was right.

"Oh, hi, Jake," Salma says, fluttering her long eyelashes at him.

"Hey," he says, brow furrowed.

"Let's go, Sal," Jess says, dragging Salma away. "See you, Roo!"

"See you . . ." I say faintly. Because now it's just me and Jake. And after the last twenty-four hours, I don't really know what to expect from him.

Neither of us says anything for a moment. I'm wondering if he's waiting for me to break the ice or if he has something he wants to say to me.

After a long, tense pause, he finally speaks. "I feel bad," he says, looking at his feet.

That's a start, I guess. But I just can't get over what Salma reported he said to Mr. Pearce! It's boggling my dehydrated, love-addled mind!

"It was only really when we got here today that I understood how stupid this whole thing was. Like . . . how ridiculous it was that I would put you in a position where you had to do this. You shouldn't have to go to all this trouble to earn my respect. That's just . . . Yeah, that's stupid. I should be able to just show you and tell you that I respect you. Not make you, like, prove to me that you can do stuff."

I nod. I mean, I agree with him! But I'm just going to let him speak.

"It was when I noticed how Sasha sees you that I realized how . . . bad I've been to you. Like, yeah, you were so much slower than everyone else, but she was just so excited that you were doing it. Anyway, I'm sorry. I should have just been, you know, supportive. The way you are with Sasha. I . . . admire it." He moves his jaw from side to side in his *thinking* pose. "I don't know why I have to be like this with you. I don't even like it. It makes me feel good for about a second and then I feel like shit. I hear myself say this stuff to you and I'm like, *Why am I saying this?*"

"You don't have to," I say, shrugging like it's no big deal. "I mean, you don't have to be nice to me all the time, but . . . you could just decide to put a stop to it now."

He doesn't say anything. He just nods.

"Anyway, calling out Mr. Pearce was a good start," I say, flushing with pride. "I know how cool you thought he was."

"He's not cool," Jake says, shaking his head. "You are." He draws me into a hug.

And then I remember. "Hey, did you know Dad was coming?"

Jake shakes his head. "He just turned up. Late, of course."

"Of course," I say, grinning.

"Maybe Mum knew. I think he's catching up on all of Sasha's gossip."

"I really want to see him. I can't believe he came," I say, craning my neck to try to find him in the thinning mass of people now that the race is over.

"Oh," Jake says, nodding over my shoulder. "There he is. I'm gonna go find Mum."

A moment later, Dad holds out his arms for a hug.

"Don't hug me—I'm too sweaty! I can only hug other sweaty people!" I protest.

"Come here," he says, pulling me close to him. He breathes in the smell of my hair, which is probably absolutely disgusting right now, but he doesn't seem to care. "God, I missed this. I missed this so much."

And even amid all my delirious happiness of finishing the race and kissing Ollie and knowing that trying to be there for Sasha isn't going unnoticed, it feels like a huge vein of sadness has opened up inside me. "I miss you so much," I say, and I can't help crying. It's like I've been holding it in all summer long, trying to avoid feeling it, trying to go out of my way so I don't have to really experience the pain of the separation from him, focusing on my anger rather than my hurt.

"I can't do it, Roo," he says, shaking his head.

"Can't do what?"

"I can't be apart from you horrible lot. I don't know what I was thinking."

"What do you mean?"

"I mean that . . . Well, what I *don't* mean is that Mum and I are getting back together because we're not. We shouldn't be together anymore. That was the right thing to do. But I just don't want to be so far away from you guys. I'm not surprised you were avoiding me for months. It's what I deserved," he says.

I frown at him, not letting myself believe what I'm hearing, not letting myself believe he's here in front of me. "So where are you going to live?"

"Oh, I don't know. It's not like there's a shortage of flats around here. I actually wanted to have a look at some over the next couple of days. Thought I would kill two birds with one stone. Find somewhere to live and come see my daughter follow in my very talented and athletic footsteps."

I roll my eyes. "Well, I wouldn't exactly call it that. I think Mr. Pearce said I had the slowest time in race history by *many* minutes."

"Nah, nah," he says, shaking his head and smiling. "None of this false modesty, Roo. I know you too well for that. You know you're a winner today. Sash thinks you're just about the coolest person in the world."

I shrug. "Well, I am. Anyway, where's Mum?"

"Over by the car," he says. "I think it's all a bit hard for her. Me being such a bastard and all."

I hug him again. "You're *our* bastard. Are you coming home with us?"

"No, but maybe I can take you all for dinner later? Real-life pizza?"

"But it's Sunday, not Wednesday!" I protest.

"Things are different now. We need new traditions, innit."

I go in search of Mum. I find her over by the car, staring into the distance.

"Mum?" I say tentatively.

She jumps. "Oh! There you are!" She wraps her arms around me. "I'm so proud of you."

"I can't believe Dad turned up. Are you feeling all right?" I say into her neck.

"Oh, don't worry about me. I'm fine. I only just got used to the idea of him being gone and now he says he's coming back. Typical," she says, but she doesn't sound bitter.

"I just wanted to say . . ." I begin, wondering what it is exactly that I want to say. "I just wanted to say thank you for never being someone who told me I couldn't do stuff. For not acting like it's obvious that someone like Ollie wouldn't like me or that I couldn't run if I wanted to. Just, you know . . . for being chill. Always."

"I can't say it ever crossed my mind to do anything different," she says, smiling but bemused.

"You just let me get on with stuff. I appreciate it."

"I appreciate you," she says, squeezing my hand. "Now, what's going on with you and Ollie? I thought teenagers were meant to go out with people their parents disapproved of!"

I blush furiously. "I don't know if I'm going out with him . . ."

"Well, don't you think you should find out?"

CHAPTER 32

"Inhale deeply through your nose . . ." Cue the sound of ten or fifteen people breathing in. "Exhale deeply through your mouth . . ." And breathing out. "Allow the gaze to come up . . ." We all raise our heads upward. "Open your eyes."

We all slowly clamber to our feet. Liv presses the button that turns off the projector. The beautiful warm, loving face of fat yoga babe Jessamyn Stanley disappears from the screen.

"That was so nice," says Heather with a dreamy smile.

"Yeah, let's do more of hers," says Ethan, stretching his long arms up so far he can almost touch the classroom ceiling.

"Thanks, Liv!" Reema calls over her shoulder as she leaves the room, balancing her yoga mat in the crook of her elbow.

Once everyone has filed out, Liv high-fives me, smiling. "How was that for another installment of the Slowpoke Running Club?"

"Not too bad! We did it again!"

"Another victory for the chill population of Dawson," she says, holding up her hand in a peace sign. "Even more chill after that *delightful* yoga class."

This is what our Wednesday afternoons look like now. Everyone has the afternoon off anyway, theoretically to do some kind of organized sport, and Liv and I wanted to find a way to make that feel . . . well, like something we might actually want to do. How about some willfully *disorganized* sport? Even though we call it the Slowpoke Running Club, we don't actually run that often. Liv and I sometimes go out together when we want some fresh air, but it's nothing like my intense summer challenge. I think that's what this has been all about for me. Finding new and different ways to move my body that don't feel goal-oriented or pressured. I've been there, done that. This is a new moment. Doing all this on my own terms. And then Liv and I wanted to open it up to other people. Hence the Slowpoke Running Club. Today it was half an hour of yoga on mats we guilted the PE department into buying for us using some spiel Liv came up with about *widening participation*.

It's for anyone. Anyone who wants to try, in a space where there is no winning or losing. Anyone who wants to move. Anyone who doesn't want to compete, doesn't *need* to compete, but wants to do it anyway. Just . . . anyone really! We're not fussy. The first week, it was only Liv and me, and every week since it's grown by a couple of people.

"Ooh, you're done!" April coos when we emerge from the classroom. "I knew I should have joined you guys today. I feel like my head is exploding with this coursework." Liv reaches over and runs her hands through April's pixie cut. April looks up at her adoringly.

Liv shrugs. "You're always welcome."

As I push open the double doors to the sixth-form block, April stands on tiptoes to kiss Liv. I can't help but smile. Two of my very favorite people in the world? Together? Hook it to my veins!

Although if April didn't have a crush on Liv before, I don't blame her for being powerless to resist after her heroism at the Dash.

The three of us go to the café down the road from school where we kill time chatting and gossiping and making one another cry with laughter over absolutely nothing until I check the time on my phone and jump into action. "Let's go!"

When we get back to school, there, freshly showered, his rugby kit slung over his shoulder, waiting for us at the entrance, is Ollie.

"There you are," he says, holding out his arms to me. I let myself be enveloped in a hug before looking up at him, into those soft, kind eyes that really *see* me, and I kiss him. Because that's what we do now. That's just what we do! It's just normal! I kiss him basically whenever I want!

"Ready for a double date?" I ask him, slipping my fingers between his. "Can you believe it? We're going on a *double date* like we're in a ye olde American film!" I say, beside myself with excitement. And why wouldn't I be beside myself with excitement these days? Ollie is my actual, literal boyfriend! And Liv is one of my very closest friends. If I hadn't taken on that challenge this summer, who knows if either of those things would have happened. And there's Jake, who's back at uni now and who I actually find myself calling for advice sometimes. Infrequently. But sometimes. Sasha still has to exist in a harsh, horrible world and I'm permanently on the lookout for ways to keep her mind the happy place it should be, but she hasn't mentioned her body to me in weeks, so I'm hopeful something's going right. And I have to say, everything feels just that little bit brighter since Dad finally moved back down here last week. It's not like he and Mum are hanging out, but it seems like a real load off everyone's mind.

As we walk to the bus stop to make our way to the cinema, I feel possessed by that same feeling I had at the end of the race. The feeling that my heart was a balloon and it was so light that I could just float away at any minute. With one hand holding Ollie's, I slip my other hand under April's arm, resting my head on her shoulder as we walk. She's holding Liv's hand. A perfect chain. As the sun sets, we walk on.

Together.

ACKNOWLEDGMENTS

Thank you to Charlotte Colwill for finding the perfect home for this book while my agent Rachel Mann was on parental leave. I couldn't have asked for a better editor than Jenny Jacoby (So wise! So precisely on my wavelength!) and a better home for it than Bonnier and Hot Key Books. Thank you to Rachel as always for her wisdom. Thank you to Beth John, Jenny Tighe, Alice Slater, Alex Smyrliadi, and Jo Bromilow for always supporting me and my writing. Thank you to Jon Cudby for being the exact kind of non-annoying Running Friend I need. Thank you to Dan Barker for letting me work in your office on the day I had the idea for *Slow Burn* and plotted it out—maybe the book wouldn't exist at all if I hadn't thought of it that specific day. Thank you to Katie Foreman for the cover design and illustration, not least because it was your first ever cover and you captured the book perfectly. Thank you to the eagle-eyed Jennie Roman for copyediting and the diligent Jane Burnard for proofreading. Thank you to Jasveen Bansal and Amber Ivatt for your help in marketing and publicizing the book, and to Holly Potter and Jessica Webb for your work on the rights and sales. Thank you as always to my family, and to Paul, forever.